ABCs
of Heartbreak

ABCs of Heartbreak

Alma Hulbert

Halo
PUBLISHING
INTERNATIONAL

Halo Publishing International
7550 WIH-10 #800, PMB 2069,
San Antonio, TX 78229

First Edition, January 2024
ISBN: 978-1-63765-537-5

The information contained within this book is strictly for informational purposes. Unless otherwise indicated, all the names, characters, businesses, places, events and incidents in this book are either the product of the author's imagination or used in a fictitious manner. Any resemblance to actual persons, living or dead, or actual events is purely coincidental.

Halo Publishing International is a self-publishing company that publishes adult fiction and non-fiction, children's literature, self-help, spiritual, and faith-based books. We continually strive to help authors reach their publishing goals and provide many different services that help them do so. We do not publish books that are deemed to be politically, religiously, or socially disrespectful, or books that are sexually provocative, including erotica. Halo reserves the right to refuse publication of any manuscript if it is deemed not to be in line with our principles. Do you have a book idea you would like us to consider publishing? Please visit www.halopublishing.com for more information.

This is for all my fellow rom-com addicts who wished they were a little more realistic and for most of Booktok; y'all are some of the most feral em-effers I've seen, and I lived through 2014 Tumblr.

Stay passionate.

CHAPTER

1

"It's gonna get better at the end; you just gotta keep pushing, you guys!" the cycling instructor yelled into his headset. A scattering of skeptical groans popcorned throughout the mirrored room, over the iconic 90s pop-rap hit playing at a capacity that rendered it unclear if it was the cycling or the bass making the mirrors quiver on the walls.

"Jesus, how long is this class again?" Mary panted just as the instructor commanded the class to do another round of push-ups. His overly energetic voice punched her in the temple with every word.

"Five minutes. Get it together; it's only a half hour long," Stacey said back in a rhythmic staccato timed to her push-ups. She took a quick second to wipe sweat from her upper lip and brow.

"I'm about to…*ahhh-tss*…*punch him,* or however this song goes," Mary grumbled.

"He's not that bad; you just need to get over the not-wanting-a-man-to-tell-you-what-to-do thing," Stacey returned. She glanced over at Mary in time to see her need-a-fill, manicured, one-finger salute.

The song came to a close, and the instructor announced the start of cooldown.

Mary sprawled her arms dramatically over the handlebars and pedaled limply to the beat of the soft strumming of a guitar. "I really need to keep up with coming to this class," she said breathlessly between gasps.

At the start of the chorus, Mary completely gave up on the cooldown, popped her shoes out of the stirrups, and *da-thump*ed onto the floor. In one stride, she was next to Stacey and mockingly swayed her fist in the air as if she were holding a lighter.

Stacey rolled her eyes and slowed her pedaling as she surrendered to a bubble of chuckles. "And how many excuses have you given me anytime I told you I was coming?"

"Umpteen plus one," Mary said with a sheepish smile.

At the end of the song, Stacey slipped off her own bike, leaned over with her hands on her knees, and groaned.

"See? I feel you shouldn't be feeling like that with all of those happy endorphins running through your body. Happy people just don't want to feel sad," Mary said.

"That's the point, ya goof." Stacey clapped her on the back and, in the rented cycling sneakers, tip-tapped across the floor and out of the room.

"Wait! You're walking like you're getting the prom crown. Slow down!" Mary yelled as she followed Stacey with an Igor limp.

"Uh, I don't think so. I want to get my reward for actually finishing the class."

* * *

The coffee shop was a comfortable level of busy for one in the Manhattan area, right down the street from Broadway; it was one of Mary's favorites because it was never ten-customers-deep busy. Plus, she got to make fun of the stereotypical-looking "artistic" hipsters with their thin wool scarf worn year-round and John Lennon-style eyeglasses.

As if on cue, her eyes landed on one all the way in the front corner of the shop. Mary nudged Stacey's arm softly as they waited in line. "Nine o'clock. They are evolving with thinking they can match that buffalo-plaid scarf with that forest-green Izod. Does he not know it's June?" Mary softly said.

Stacey, less than obviously, rolled her head to the side and made a display of shivering in disgust once she saw him. They fell into a fit of giggles while they ordered, waited, and finally sat by the side windows.

Mary slumped over and rested her forehead on the table with a soft *thunk*.

Stacey patted her on the head as she took a sip of her iced coffee. "It'll be okay. You survived in time for another trip to get coffee, so that's a plus in my book," Stacey said.

"Yeah, because I'm sure you'd marry coffee before you'd marry Tyler," Mary said to her lap.

"Please, we're already married. I'll just have to break the news to Tyler when he does propose to me."

Mary's head popped up, and she took a quick swig of coffee before taking a dramatic, deep breath. "Do you know when he'll do it?" She put her chin in a finger hammock and fluttered her eyelashes expectantly.

"It has to be any day now. He told me he set a dinner reservation for next Wednesday because we both have off, and he went shopping with his friend Abby a couple of weeks ago. I kind of hope he replicates one of our first dates for it, to make it a little special, like maybe to the arcade after dinner or something."

"I'm sure, if you suggest it, he might just take you anyway. Also, doesn't he normally go shopping with her? They've been friends for years before he met you."

"Well, yeah, but when I asked if he was getting anything good, he just said he was going to Macy's for a couple of things. He never said what, and he said he couldn't find anything he liked when he came home afterward."

"Or he made the mistake of going to Macy's in the first place because they don't have anything good in their jewelry department anymore." Mary took a sip with her pinky up and looked away as if she were a tea-sipping frog.

"You also don't like rings, to begin with, so you can't say anything."

Mary looked down at her hands and slowly nodded in casual agreement. "You're right, and when you're right, you're right. And that's all the time!" Mary said sarcastically, with a tip of her imaginary fedora.

"Thank you, peasant," Stacey said with the worst-possible posh British accent.

Mary snorted loudly and accidentally shot a missile of snot onto her arm.

An older woman at the table next to them gave them a disgusted once-over.

"Don't be saucy with me!" Mary said to the woman in an exaggerated posh accent of her own.

Stacey tried to hold in her laughter, failed miserably, and brought her head down to the table in an attempt to hide how red her face had become.

The older woman harrumphed into her paper cup as she stood up and walked out.

Mary burst into laughter as soon as the door was closed.

Stacey whipped her head back up to wipe the tears from her eyes, and she recovered just enough to get out, "I knew it. I'm surrounded by idiots."

Mary almost fell out of her chair, shaking from her silent laughter, and Stacey turned beet red from trying to keep back a fresh flood of giggles.

"Can you two *not* with this shit again?" one of the baristas yelled at them.

They looked over at him and saw he was forcing himself to keep a smile off his face, as if he'd overheard their entire conversation, but the look on his manager's face behind him was anything but patient. So they grabbed their cups and zigzagged their way out of the front door, still laughing.

* * *

"Give me a call when you make it home," Stacey said to Mary, who was still sitting in the back of the air-conditioned PT Cruiser Uber. A fresh drop of sweat beaded on Stacey's temple as she adjusted her purse on her shoulder.

"Girl, it's 3:00 p.m., and it's, like, three blocks away. I'll be fine. Unless Becky wants to get frisky." Mary waggled her eyebrows at the driver suggestively.

"Flattering, but I'm good," Stacey heard the driver say monotonically. Mary mockingly mimed the driver's words to Stacey with a roll of her eyes, and Stacey let out a snort.

After they waved their goodbyes, Stacey hiked up the stairs, each step burning her calves a degree higher than the last. When she finally made it to her apartment door, she glanced down to make sure the skin hadn't started to melt off her legs.

She opened the door to her third-floor apartment and immediately went to the sink for a quick glass of water. With a post-gym, tired sigh and body parts she didn't know could throb in sync with her heartbeat, she walked with a bit of a wobble to her bedroom to grab her towel for a shower.

She opened the door to see the naked back of Tyler and hear a feminine voice breathlessly say, "Shit."

Tyler quickly pulled away from the girl and gaped at Stacey like a deer in the headlights. "Oh shit, Stacey. No, no, no. Oh God," he stammered so quickly that each word blended into the next as if they made up one big word.

"What the fu—" Stacey began, but stopped abruptly as the girl grappled at the sheet to try to cover herself, and Stacey caught a glimpse of her face. "Abby? Are you fucking kidding me?!" Stacey screamed, and angry tears trickled down her cheeks before she realized she was crying.

"Stacey, I'm sorry. I—" Tyler began, but Stacey turned and double-stepped to the front door in a blind fog, directed only by muscle memory of the apartment that she had shared with Tyler for the last two and a half years. She heard footsteps behind her, but each one of their steps propelled her closer to the door. She burst through the door and was already at the landing of the second floor by the time whoever was following her caught up.

"Stacey, wait. I'm so sorry. Stacey, stop!"

She skidded to a stop and threw her head back to look over her shoulder and see Tyler leaning over the banister, with just a towel—HER towel—around his waist. She glared up toward him, but it took a few hard blinks to clear the tears from her vision.

His mixed expression of fear and surprise began to take on a red hue as her blood started to boil and crawl its way to her cheeks. "What? What the fuck could you possibly say right now? 'Don't go; I'm so sorry; I didn't mean to?" she yelled up at him in a mocking tone, complete with her hands on her hips and leaning a little at her waist. "Jesus fucking Christ, that's some bullshit, and you know it."

"It was an accident! She came over, and we got to talking—" he started, but his eyes began to fly back and forth as he looked for a way to finish his excuse.

"Do you hear yourself right now? Obviously not, because your dick was talking louder than your brain."

"Stacey, come the fuck on. It was an accident," Tyler yelled down in an exasperated tone.

The sudden change in his tone and demeanor took her by surprise, and she physically took a small step back to regain her balance. "Fucking another person isn't an accident; you have—" she began, but Tyler interrupted her.

He placed his hand on his hip and started talking over her. "Yeah, it's definitely not an accident when I get tired of your boring-ass shit. Fuck, Stacey, you need to get the fuck over yourself. I have needs!"

Stacey chuckled humorlessly. "Needs? You had a girlfriend living with you; you had a shit ton of chances where you could 'fulfill your needs,' whatever the fuck that means," she said with finger quotes. Once she finished, she crossed her arms.

Tyler shifted the weight on his feet so he could pop his hip to the side.

Just then, a dog in the apartment closest to Stacey began to bark and scratch at the door, and from somewhere on the fourth floor, a creaky door opened. A woman with a laundry basket in her hands and headphones over her ears stopped short when she looked over the banister. Her eyes landed on Tyler in the towel first and then down at Stacey with her gym-makeup look streaming down her cheeks. The woman rolled her eyes and turned back around, loudly muttering to herself about there always being drama somewhere.

Stacey looked back at Tyler, whose face grew more exasperated by the second, and she couldn't figure out where one emotion of her own started and the next one ended as a flood of betrayal, hatred, and the first shattering of a broken heart trickled through her. She blinked a few times to clear her vision, and that's when she saw it; his eyes rolled, and his lips slightly parted as he let out a tired sigh full of words she realized she didn't want to hear.

She took a cleansing breath, trying to relax the tension building up in her throat before it took her over completely, and croaked out one word, "Why?"

His shoulders slumped, and he rested his arms on the banister casually after running his hand through his hair. His eyes darted around while his mouth gaped like a fish in a theatrical attempt to put his words together.

"You've gotten boring. Honestly, you've been a little boring since the beginning, but I figured it would get better over time. And it's in every sense of the word; your hobbies...or lack of them...your storytelling abilities, which only made the lame things that happened to you more lame, your same-three sex positions. But I couldn't hold that against you because you've only ever been with a few other..."

Tyler continued to speak, but Stacey's ears started to ring with an echo of blood rushing through her veins that hushed him out. Stiffly, she turned on her heel and walked down the other flight of stairs and out of the lobby.

* * *

"Listen, bitch, I told you, you tired me out, and I just want to take a nap," Mary said through the intercom.

Stacey didn't move or say anything in response.

"Is this even Stacey? Yes, it's you," Mary answered herself after she looked out her kitchen window. "Why didn't you just call me, you goof? I'll be down in a minute."

The intercom buzzed off.

A minute later, Mary pushed open the door and looked quizzically at Stacey, who was still looking at the intercom. "Stace? I'm here; you can come in now."

Stacey turned her head, and Mary's stomach fell when she saw her puffy eyes.

"Stace? What happened?"

"Tyler—" she began, but sobs took the place of her words.

Mary pulled her into a hug, and Stacey sobbed into her shoulder. "Come in, hon. Come on."

Mary pulled her into the building and walked her over to her apartment. Once the door closed behind them, Stacey leaned over, placed her hands on her knees, and let out one loud sob. Mary rubbed Stacey's back until her breathing started to even out. Then Stacey slowly stood up straight and wordlessly looked at Mary.

"What happened, Stace?"

Stacey's eyes fluttered over to the couch, and Mary took the hint and directed her to it. After she took a couple more breaths, and after two attempts to begin, Stacey recounted everything that happened.

"What the fuck?! What the actual fuck? That mother-fucker. I'm gonna castrate him. I'm gonna rip one of her tits off."

Even though every breath chipped off another piece of her heart, Stacey couldn't help but chuckle a little at Mary's extreme courses of action. "She doesn't have much, so you might be ripping off the whole boob, honestly," Stacey managed to say.

CHAPTER
2

Onyx tonight at 9:30, Mary texted Stacey a week later in the middle of the fourth irate call she received that morning. The magazine she worked for, *Econ-Living*, had recently raised their retail price, which happened to affect subscriptions in a way they hadn't foreseen: double-billing subscribers in one month. Since the magazine was still on the small side, with one floor of employees and an out-sourced printing service, she was stuck helping answer phones in an attempt at crowd control.

She unmuted the call and began to tell the woman on the other end of the phone that the company did indeed send out notification that the price would go up, but the exact date of when the increase would go into effect had not been determined at the time. Stacey omitted that last part, knowing it wouldn't go over that well.

The woman went off, and Stacey muted the call once more. She turned to Kelly, her rear-cubicle buddy and the clear-thinking friend between Mary and her. Stacey shook her head slightly as she watched Kelly speed swiping left on her phone while the company phone blinked silently.

"Onyx tonight at nine thirty."

"Mary already texted me."

"God dammit, Mary," Stacey whispered.

"But I'm there. It's been a hot minute since I've had a drink, and it may be my last chance to go out with you guys before I move next week," Kelly said.

"Chicago doesn't know what it's in for," Stacey said.

Kelly threw a pen at her in response. "Want me to come over, and we can pick out a couple of outfits between the three of us?" Kelly asked after a few more left swipes.

"I feel like Mary already had our outfits picked out as soon as she sent that text."

"Has it been that long since you've gone out?"

"A little bit, but her form of getting over someone means she is going to just push me to get back out there, even if that means I'm just wearing nipple pasties."

"Knowing her, she'll do it to you too. 'Op, hang on," Kelly said.

Their boss Steve was making his rounds around the floor and had been on high alert ever since the first complaint the day before. She picked up the phone and robotically greeted the caller. Within a second of being on the phone, Kelly pulled the headset away from her ear and dramatically winced.

"Are you even listening to me, young lady!" the woman screamed into Stacey's phone.

She flinched, dropped the phone in surprise and embarrassment at having forgotten about the caller, and clicked it off mute once more. "I understand your frustration, ma'am. I was just looking into your account to verify your concern, but if you would like, I can transfer you to my supervisor."

"Yeah, as long as they are more polite than you and actually know what they are doing at their job."

"Please stay on the line, ma'am, while I transfer you," Stacey said robotically. She transferred the call to Greg, who sat two seats down from her, and stared him down as she waited for him to pick up.

He gave her a confused "What?" when he realized she was staring at him and looked at his phone in annoyance a moment later. He answered; a couple of exchanges later, he raised his hand and flipped the bird in her direction.

Stacey chuckled to herself and leaned back in her chair as she watched the show.

From her inconveniently placed position between Greg and her, Lisa turned in her chair and gave Stacey a condescending smile. "You know he can get in trouble if he fucks that call up," Lisa said, looking down her nose at Stacey.

"What? We're friends. We've been going back and forth like that for a while. Besides, it's just another annoying caller complaining about the bill. I'm sure he's had a few of those already today."

"If he isn't here at the end of the day, you'll have yourself to blame," Lisa said. She turned back to her computer as if to say that was the end of the conversation.

Behind Lisa's back, Stacey bit her thumb. Kelly stifled a laugh, and Stacey held in the bubble of laughter of her own as her phone started to ring for the sixth time, all before having her second cup of coffee.

* * *

"You aren't pregaming hard enough," Mary said. She stood in the door of her bathroom, looking over Kelly and Stacey as they put on their makeup and fixed their hair, respectively.

Kelly threw her makeup sponge at her. "We are classy ladies in New York City; we do not pregame and get sloshed before going out."

"But New York City is expensive. Fifteen dollars for a fucking screwdriver using vodka that practically still has chunks of potato in it? Fuck you kindly." She looked into the mirror as if it were a camera on *The Office*.

24

"You do have a point. You have some more of that cereal-flavored vodka?" Stacey asked.

"Thought you'd never ask."

As Stacey wandered out of the bathroom and toward Mary's fridge, there was a soft knock on the door. She turned to the doorway and saw Krista in skintight, black, ripped skinny jeans, black-lace bralette, and Converses. A smile crept over Stacey's lips as she almost jumped into Krista's arms. "Krista!" she shrilled.

Krista matched her energy and actually went in for a hug.

"Mary, your boo thang is here!" Stacey yelled from over Krista's shoulder. She pulled away and looked over to see Mary casually bouncing between the bathroom and bedroom as she gave them a simple "What's up?" wave.

"I feel like it's a bad sign that I'm more excited to see your girlfriend than you are."

"Woman, I am looking for the earrings that will be the *pièce de résistance* of this outfit, and you just don't appreciate good taste!" Clatter echoed from Mary's bedroom, followed by an exasperated grunt.

Krista hit Override and entered Mom mode. She helped Mary look for an earring after a quick kiss break before continuing on.

Twenty minutes, an epic search for a lost earring, and three shots each later, they stepped out onto the sidewalk and into the stagnant, cooling June night air. They walked a block and turned a corner toward their regular bar. The buzz of people laughing and melodic guitar riffs of whatever was playing on the app-controlled jukebox drifted toward them before they were even able to see the establishment.

A couple of strides later, Stacey stopped short in the middle of the sidewalk, staring at the crack in the concrete at her feet. Kelly slowed a little, Mary took a couple more steps, but it took Krista kiddie leashing Stacey's hand before she realized what was happening.

"I don't know if I'm ready for this," Stacey said through her thickening throat. She leaned over, put her hands on her knees, and watched a teardrop fall from the tip of her nose to the sidewalk.

Kelly began to rub her back, and Mary rolled her eyes. "How do you know if you aren't ready for it if you don't even make it to the bar?" she asked, slurring her words.

Kelly shot her a glare, but Mary just shrugged her shoulders.

After some cleansing breaths, Stacey stood up and took a few wobbly steps of her own through the night.

CHAPTER

3

Mary's blender revved to life with what must have been a nail smoothie and woke Stacey up mid-snore. She coughed for two straight minutes, trying to get her breathing back to some semblance of normal. Once she pulled in that last cleansing breath, the pain in her throat quickly moved to her head and pulsed with every heartbeat.

"Mare," Stacey said softly, trying to get her vocal cords to work. "Mare," she tried again after clearing her throat, but the blender still rumbled on. Stacey tried a few more times, attempting to get a little louder every time.

The blender finally turned off, and a deafening silence followed for a moment before she heard a muttered, "Always when I'm making something." Stacey let out a one-breath chuckle and regretted it the moment it happened because it felt as if her eyes were about to pop out of her head.

"You rang?" Mary said as she popped her head into the bedroom.

"Must you make smoothies this early in the morning?"

"Girl, it is 11:00 a.m. And you and I both know full goddamn well you spent the other half of the night in the bathroom, praying to the porcelain gods," Mary said, raising an "you know I'm right" eyebrow.

Stacey replied with a sheepish, White-person cheek smile and rolled onto her back. She ran her tongue over her teeth, and the acidic grime reminded her just how long she had spent in the bathroom. A wave of nausea hit her for a split second, and she had to take a deep breath to help it pass.

"That's what I thought," Mary said, as if reading Stacey's mind.

"But, still, fucking smoothies?"

"You need your nutrients; don't give me that. I'd say go brush your teeth, but I used orange juice as a base."

"Yes, Mom," Stacey mumbled as she rolled away from Mary. She heard the tip-tap sound of bare feet on hardwood fade in the direction of the kitchen, and after some shuffling and clattering on the counter, it seemed as if Mary was thankfully done with the blending.

When Stacey finally felt that she could keep her eyes open without feeling as if her brain were going to explode, she shuffled herself out into the living room and plopped down at one end on the couch, her legs taking up the middle cushion. Mary was on the other end, and she handed Stacey a glass. Even though the thought of eating at that moment repulsed her, Stacey took a tiny sip. The ice-cold orange and pineapple felt so good on her throat that she took a couple of gulps.

"That a girl. You'll become a functioning human again in no time."

"How do you make such good fucking smoothies, Mare?"

"Practice and stealing from ex-girlfriends. You remember Rebecca?"

"The health nut that got you into cycling?"

"Yeah. She kinda let slip her secret recipe for smoothies, so I guess I actually got something good out of that relationship."

"Besides the fact that she was extremely flexible," Stacey stated.

"That's beside the point," Mary said with a wave of her hand, as if clearing smoke out of her face.

Stacey lightly kicked Mary, and they both laughed into their smoothies. When Stacey finally finished hers, she tipped her head back onto the armrest and yawned.

"None of that," Mary said as she slapped Stacey's feet.

"You, out of the four of us that went out, know best how my night ended, so I think it's understood that I deserve a yawn or two."

"Don't remind me. Do you actually remember last night?" Mary asked.

Embarrassment washed over Stacey in a scalding flash; her cheeks instantly caught fire. "Yeah. I was bad, but I still remember that I danced with a guy last night." Stacey shivered in disgust when her memory brought into focus just how hard her beer goggles had been working.

"Girl, I think the worst part was when he was creepily watching you try to twerk. He proceeded to circle the floor around you, and literally jumped down from the edge of the dance floor to grind up on you. And you didn't even care!"

"Wait! He was watching me like a hawk before he went in for the kill? Why didn't you push him off of me?"

"Because you locked lips with him before we had the chance."

Stacey groaned in disappointment with herself and lightly banged her head on the armrest.

"Don't beat yourself up too much, kid; you'll throw up all over my rug."

"Wouldn't be called a throw rug for nothing then," Stacey retorted, finishing it off with a couple of finger guns.

Mary lightly slapped Stacey's foot. "Just shut up and drink your damn smoothie, wiseass."

* * *

Bright and early Monday morning, Stacey walked onto the eighth floor, clomped over to her cubicle, and plopped her purse down onto the desk.

Lisa dramatically gave her a sideways glare and just shook her head as she turned back to her own computer screen.

"Can I help you, Lisa? I'm not particularly in the mood for being told I look like shit. I do have mirrors at home."

"Well, damn, I guess I won't tell you I saw you at Onyx the other night," Lisa said without looking back at her.

A chilling rush of embarrassment flooded up Stacey's neck, Looney Tunes-style. Daffy Duck would be so proud. "Oh God," she said, deflated. She plopped down into her computer chair and limply started to log into the computer.

"Yep. Who was that you were dancing with?"

"Well, it definitely wasn't anyone I knew or wanted to know. They make the drinks pretty strong there."

"Someone say something about drinks?" Greg said from over his one-foot-tall corkboard divider on the other side of Lisa.

"Yes, Gamma Phi, we are talking about drinks," Lisa threw over her shoulder.

"I may have gone to a private college, but I wasn't ever in a fraternity. And, besides, I feel like that was actually the sorority on my campus," Greg shot back with an air of faux hurt.

"Whatever. I was trying to know who Stacey was dancing with and when the wedding was gonna be."

Lisa gave her signature snotty-gossip grin that Stacey wanted to slap off her face every time she made it. Instead, Stacey just opened up her Outlook.

"Wait! Don't you have a boyfriend?" Greg asked.

Stacey looked at him, and he started to blur as her eyes smoked over as her tears started to put out the flames that had resided in them a moment ago.

Lisa spun in her chair and gave Greg a full-on sigh of impatience. "They broke up last week. You would know that if you weren't always mentally on vacation."

"Oh shit, Stacey. I'm sorry to hear that. You guys seemed really good together," Greg said softly.

"Well, not as good together as you thought because he went after his best friend," Stacey shot at him.

Greg seemed taken back for a moment, but then he shook his head slowly. "Men are dogs. And I can say that because I was a tool back in college. But that was college, and we are grown adults now. There really isn't a reason for it at this point. So fuck him," Greg said. He gave Stacey a lopsided grin of understanding.

Stacey found herself returning one of gratitude. When she had the thought that maybe Greg was a better guy than he had always led them to believe, she snapped herself back down to the office and lightly slapped her thighs as a sign that she was about to make an announcement.

"On that lovely note, we should maybe get started actually working while we are all gathered here," Stacey said a bit too chipper.

With a bored shoulder shrug, Lisa turned back to her computer as she muttered, "Not quite at that level, but whatever."

Greg gave Stacey a quick head nod. They locked eyes for a second, and the tiniest butterfly made its presence known in her stomach. As she looked at her screen begrudgingly, she found twenty unread emails. Her mind began overthinking everything, wondering what his look might have meant. She caught herself thinking about it multiple times throughout the day and had to force herself to keep her mind on her work; that happened more times than she would have liked.

* * *

"Aaand that's 5:00 p.m.!" Greg announced from his computer. He had already packed up his things and was standing. Lisa followed suit quickly after and started to walk out as soon as her purse was over her shoulder.

Stacey turned off her computer, and when she stood to tuck her own purse into her elbow, she saw Greg was still standing behind his desk, watching her.

He scratched the back of his head and cleared his throat. "Are you up to anything right now?" he asked. He cleared his throat once more.

"I was more than likely just going to go home and have some Pinot Grigio for dinner, if I'm being honest."

"What would you say to having Pinot Grigio *with* dinner with someone who was planning to do the same?" Greg asked, avoiding Stacey's eyes and stealing glances in her direction to gauge her reaction.

She had three emotions run through her all at once and decided incredulous and annoyed were rude, so she went with curious. She reviewed a couple of responses in her head and finally decided on playful to lighten the mood. "I didn't know you liked Pinot Grigio," she said, and was happy to see that he went from worried to pleasantly surprised.

"Not particularly, I'm in too deep with beer to give it up quite yet." He gave her that half grin, and the butterfly seemed to invite some friends.

* * *

"Is this a spot you usually go to?" Stacey asked when they walked into the hole-in-the-wall bar that was literally in the basement of a five-story walk-up a couple of blocks from their office building.

"Yeah, it's on the way home from work, so I'll usually meet up with buddies on Thursdays here."

"Not Fridays? I'd figure you wouldn't want to worry about drinking too much the night before work."

"As much shit as you and Lisa give me for seeming like a stereotypical frat guy—who was never in a frat, by the way, because apparently you guys haven't heard that bit yet—I'm an adult and only have a beer here and there. Besides, Thursday night is Trivia Night," he said sheepishly and began to turn red as he was saying it.

Stacey's lips quirked up a little on one side. "I didn't know you were a nerd!" Stacey teased.

Greg grimaced as she punched him in the arm as if he was just a buddy. But he quickly replaced it with another grin. "I'm actually pretty good. Who would have thought that having a mother who's such a fan of the groovy 70s and a father who was an accountant for a chain of grocery stores would have taught me all sorts of obscure old pop culture and math tricks."

"I am impressed. I think I'll have to come some night to see if you really walk the walk you talk."

"I would have to persuade you not to because, when I do happen to have a couple of drinks, I tend to get a little too friendly."

"All the more reason," Stacey said. She was suddenly hit with regret and embarrassment, and she slapped her hand over her mouth. "Oh my God, I have no idea why I just said that. It seemed like the appropriate answer, but I should have said something like, 'That still sounds like fun.' Oh God." She stumbled over her words to try to get out all her thoughts and backtracking, but his laughter started to drown her babbling.

"No, that's okay because I was going to say something along the same lines. Only I was going to wait a little longer before I said it."

His admission made Stacey stop short and gave her a chance to look at his face. She started to see not only the friendly and standard Ivy League frat look about him, but also how he had *the* sharpest jaw, light-brown eyes that flickered with a hint of hazel, and biceps that actually bulged through his dress shirt oh-so subtly when he bent his arms or flexed his muscles.

She looked up to see that he was looking her over with a hint of desire that flashed in his eyes when they lingered over her chest. When their eyes met, she had a moment of hesitation. *Did* she want to? Did *he* want to? *Why* did she want to? And then she was hit with the realization that she had actually wanted to hook up with him for a while, but her loyal mind had kept those thoughts at bay because she was a fucking adult who knew how to commit to a relationship.

"Should we pay for our drinks, or would you like another one?" Greg asked to break the silence that had fallen between them.

"Pay. How far away did you say you lived?"

* * *

They walked up just one flight of stairs—to Stacey's delight after the five-block walk they just had—and Greg motioned for her to step in before him. The very first thing she saw caught her by surprise—a sectional, in a deep-charcoal color, facing a beautiful, modern-style entertainment system, and not a crushed beer can in sight. There were a couple of different types of gaming controllers on his coffee table, but not a single stray sock or plate. She heard Greg chuckle beside her, and she looked up to see he was just a foot away from her, causing her to awkwardly crane her head up suddenly to look at his face.

"You were expecting a pong table or some nudie mags?" He walked over to the fridge and pulled out a bottle of beer and a lime-flavored hard seltzer. "Is this all right?"

"Grapefruit is usually my first choice, but this is still good. But I was expecting more like beer cans and laundry. Oh, there it is," she said as she turned and saw a full sink of dishes next to a full drain rack.

"That's possibly one of the few bad traits I kept from college." He took a sip from his bottle, holding the neck with just one finger, and watched as she followed suit.

"And what would one of the other bad traits be?" she asked.

He set his bottle on the kitchen table next to her and suddenly towered over her. "I wouldn't say it's a bad trait, but it goes something like this," he said as his hand lightly trailed to the nape of her neck, and he pulled her into a kiss.

It was soft at first, but his heat and height—and as much as she didn't want to admit it, his masculine and musky smell—drove her to grab the back of his head and hold him to her.

His other hand found the zipper to her dress on the first attempt, and he slowly pulled it down, stopping at her bra to pull it aside. They inspected each other's face in the same heated frenzy, waiting impatiently for the other to make the first move to continue. Stacey was the one to break the tension by pulling his lips back down to hers.

He pulled the zipper the rest of the way a little too fast, and it caught on the waistband of her panties. "Shit," he mumbled against her lips.

She pulled away and tried to free the panties from the zipper, but seemed to only make things worse. Before he gave her a defeated groan, she pushed the dress down over her hips, taking the panties with it.

"That was kinda hot," he said.

She snapped her bra off as he removed his shirt to reveal a once-athletic, but now comfortably soft body that matched his buff-when-flexing arms. She helped him unbutton his pants, but distracted him with another kiss; he broke it just long enough to kick out of his underwear. His hands lightly gripped her hips, and she could feel him start to push her toward the bedroom. She grabbed his hand, spun around, and pulled him behind her.

CHAPTER

4

"Shut the fuck up; you did not!" Mary slapped the kitchen table.

Stacey gave her a little shrug and a sly grin; then she stood up and walked to the fridge. She pulled out a hard cider and took a few exaggerated gulps, knowing Mary was staring her down, telepathically trying to tell her to continue the story. She walked over to the couch and plopped on her end; Mary was at the other end with her bowl of pasta the next time she blinked.

"I did."

"Girl, I knew he's wanted to jump your bones for the longest time. It was written all over his face, even when we ran into him at Target that one time. Was he good at least?"

"The first time, yeah," Stacey said, purposely nonchalant, and kept a playful and expectant eye on Mary for her reaction.

As if on cue, Mary almost choked on her rotini. "How many times did you do it?"

"Just twice, but I think he needed a little longer to recuperate than he led on, so he was kinda at half-mast most of the time. Tyler was worse; he couldn't go more than once in, like, a twelve-hour span."

"That should have been your first sign that Tyler was a piece of shit, inside and out," Mary said.

Stacey gave a noncommittal shrug to make it look as if just hearing his name didn't bother her, and she took another sip of her cider. "I also have a hole in my panties because of it. Thankfully, they weren't one of my cuter ones."

Mary coughed out a rotini and had to set her bowl on the coffee table so she could grab on to the couch to brace herself for whatever Stacey had to say next.

With a sigh and a casual dismissal flick of the wrist in the air, Stacey said, "He was pulling the zipper of my dress down, and it got caught on my underwear."

The matter-of-fact tone crushed the anticipation that had built within Mary, as if she'd received a blow to the head with an Acme anvil. In retaliation, she threw the closest pillow she could find at Stacey. "That was some cheap shit. I was ready for some jungle-man aggression shit."

"That turns you on?"

"Straight girls watch gay porn. Why can't I watch straight porn?" Mary said.

Stacey let that soak in for a second, and then she just nodded her head in acceptance and drank the rest of the bottle.

"So how did you guys leave things?"

Stacey thought about it for a second, and a flush of worry washed down her spine when she realized she would have to face Greg at work the next day. "I guess we're fine. We didn't really talk about it, but I think it's understood that it was a one-time thing. Oh God, what if Lisa finds out? I would be so fucked."

"Yo, fuck Lisa. That priss needs to get fucked more than you do. If she wasn't so fucking catty, though, I would help her out with it," Mary said with a suggestive and very poorly done eyebrow wiggle.

Stacey threw the pillow right back at her. "Please! Don't ever do that again…ever. It's creepy as hell."

* * *

Stacey stepped off the elevator and peered around the corner toward her cubicle; she saw that Greg was there, talking with Lisa. He didn't seem to be into whatever she was saying, but hopefully he was distracted enough to not say anything to her when she walked over.

"Look what the cat dragged in," Lisa announced as Stacey dropped her purse onto her desk.

"Happy Tuesday to you too?" Stacey said.

"You really need to figure out how to get more sleep because I'm pretty sure death has been looking better than you lately."

"Lisa, can you fuck off with your comments today? No one actually cares about what you have to say," Stacey snapped.

Lisa visibly seemed thrown off, as if she couldn't believe someone would stop her mid-rant. "That's exactly what I'm talking about. You'd have a better personality if you got some sleep."

"And you would be a civil human being if you had some dick."

Greg stifled a laugh, but the strained sound that rose out of Lisa's throat drowned it out. A few heads from the cluster of cubicles across the way popped up to see who was choking their cat in the middle of the office.

"At least when I snag a man, he isn't tempted to screw around," Lisa shot back.

Stacey's jaw dropped, and her hand shook as she restrained herself from slapping Lisa.

Lisa gave her a satisfied and rather smug smile before she walked away.

Tears began to prickle in Stacey's eyes, and her throat started to close in on itself. She slumped into her chair and turned away from Greg and the other onlookers before any tears could kamikaze in front of them. She pretended to do some work until she heard someone sit in the chair on the other side of her.

"You okay?" Greg asked softly.

She gave him a soft nod and failed to catch a tear before it fell onto the desk.

"You're not okay," he answered for her. "Did you take any days off after the breakup?"

"No."

"Maybe you should have. You can see if you can take a couple of PTO days. God knows, it would be best to get as far away from the train wreck that calls herself Lisa as you can," Greg said.

Stacey chuckled softly and wiped away another tear. "I'm fine. I promise. Besides, if everyone took a day or two after a breakup, there would barely be five people working at any given time."

"I guess you're right. Let me know if you need help getting things off your mind."

Stacey's heart fluttered for a second when she realized that was possibly another invitation to hook up. She nodded a couple of times to give herself time to form a response.

"Get a couple of drinks in me, and I'll have a more defini-
tive answer."

* * *

That afternoon at lunch, Stacey wandered out to the
corner coffee shop to grab a muffin to see if eating something would help settle her stomach. As she waited in line,
she looked at the small stack of magazines set up to calm
impatient customers like her. Her eyes roamed over the
basic structure of different magazines displaying bathing
suits, oiled pecs, and plunging-neckline power suits sans
button-up and bra. Her eyes hovered on her guilty-plea-
sure magazine, and a headline on the front.made her pull
it out of the rack and buy it.

Once she sat down with her muffin, iced tea, and magazine, she flipped through to see what the article was about.

> *The ABCs of Heartbreak*
>
> *We have all been there, staring at that rom-
> com through teary eyes, eating a box of chocolates*
> Legally Blonde-*style. But instead of throwing
> away the box and wasting any raspberry-filled
> chocolates, check out this list of some dos and
> don'ts of postpartum from your ex-bae.*

The *Legally Blonde* reference was almost too overdone,
but the movie itself was still a classic. She read down the

list of objects and activities listed in alphabetical order and some of the dos and don'ts surrounding them.

We are all adults here, and we all know that A *is for alcohol. This isn't* Sesame Street, *but there are still some lessons we'll need to teach you. DO: Have some girl-power happy hours because your posse is THE best source of positive vibes after you've lost all that dead weight. DON'T: It is possible to turn to alcohol to make everything seem a bit better, and once you start thinking,* I have more at home after I finish my second round of two-for-one happy-hour drinks, *you may need to have a talk with your girlfriends.*

Stacey was a little taken aback at the juxtaposition between the dos and don'ts throughout the list; it seemed as if there were two completely different people in charge of the two. She skimmed the article and saw that the *B* was for beaches, *C* was for cuddles, and *D* was for dancing. She read on to see if there was anything that wasn't so cliche, and then she landed on the *L*.

L is for lists, and this may be the best thing for you to do to get your mind off of things when things seem to get a little dark. DO: Self-explanatory—make a list. It could focus on a specific topic or just be a random doodle, Robert California from The Office-*style. Start off with something simple, such as your favorite desserts or dream jobs or animals that start with the same letter as your name. Bonus round if it's a to-do list of sorts, and you finish it because you're a bad bitch. DON'T: Make a hit list. It's not cute, and it's really creepy. Just don't do it.*

Stacey thought about maybe starting a list of her own, but kept drawing a blank on what it would focus around, so she skimmed through the rest of the article and was both excited and annoyed that they ended it with a "What, like it's hard?" She rolled the magazine up, threw it into her purse, and walked out with her half-eaten muffin in hand.

* * *

The door to Mary's apartment opened with a sudden slam against the wall that made Stacey drop the piece of bacon back into the grease-filled pan, hot oil splattering her wrist. "Shit!" she growled as she ran her wrist under cold water.

"Will it make you feel better that I think it smells fantastic?" Mary asked sheepishly.

"Maybe. Tell me what made you so happy," Stacey said as she dried her hands.

Mary closed her eyes and brought her hands up to her lips as if she were praying, took a deep breath, and yelled, "I'm getting a promotion!"

Stacey dropped the towel and started screaming along with Mary. She quickly turned the bacon off after it splattered the back of her arm, and she ran over to Mary to give her a hug. "That's amazing! When did this happen? I didn't think they had any more room for lead interior designers."

"That's the thing; the other Mary got canned because she kept insisting that modern was not better, and it was driving clients away from the business altogether. So they gave it to me!"

"It's about time! You've been a lowly team member for how long now? Five years?"

"Tell me about it," Mary said.

Stacey ran to the fridge, pulled out two bottles of hard cider, and made a little toast to Mary.

After they both had a couple of sips, Mary sat in one of the kitchen chairs and slammed her fists down as if she were holding utensils. "Bring my dinner, servant."

"You're going to get some of this bacon grease if you keep that up."

Mary waved her off; mid-sip, she remembered something and almost spit everything out. "So how was work today with Greg?"

"It was fine with Greg; he actually had to console me after Lisa went for the throat." Stacey gave her a rundown of the horrid adventures of Lisa while she finished making the eggs and toast.

"That bitch. That's a new low, even for her. And it sounds like Greg is a little too cool with the hookup."

"What do you mean, 'too cool'?"

"The fact that he was able to let you know that he wants to do it again in such a natural way. It seems like he's gotten pretty good about sliding in, pun fully intended."

Stacey took a bite of her toast and gave a couple of slow and thoughtful chews before answering, "I guess so. Honestly, I don't know how I was so levelheaded about the whole thing. Lord knows, I still have no idea what I'm doing when it comes to guys."

"Yeah, well, that says more about the three guys you've been with than you, if you think about it, especially if two of them were for two or so years."

"Hey, I've been with four guys! Remember that one that we played cornhole with at the bar the summer I met Tyler?"

"Oh shit, that's right! The one who you hooked up with not once, but twice, at his friend's place instead of his own. Shit, what was his name?"

"Uhhh…Adam. But I will admit he was damn good with his tongue." Stacey wiggled her eyebrows suggestively at Mary, and Mary threw the last bite of her bacon at her in retaliation.

Mary washed the dishes while Stacey plopped down on the couch, magazine in hand, to look at the "That's Just Rude" section and to see what weird fashion trend they were trying to show off this time without making it look as if they'd pulled it directly from a magazine from the seventies.

"Hey, shocker—they are trying to make striped, ribbed shirts in marigold-yellow and brown under overalls a thing again," Stacey yelled to Mary over the rushing of the water splashing in the sink.

Mary turned the water off and walked over while drying her hands. "What was that?"

"The seventies are trying to make a comeback this year." Stacey showed the magazine to Mary reading-circle style.

Mary scoffed loudly. "That's—what?—the third year in a row?"

"Not including the actual years in the seventies, sounds about right."

Mary walked back into the kitchen and opened up the fridge. "Want another cider?"

"Is there any more of that grapefruit Kolsch from upstate?"

"Sorry to disappoint."

"Then, yeah, I'll take another one."

Stacey heard clinks and two satisfying fizzes, and suddenly felt Mary plop next to her while she was focusing on letter *M* in the magazine list.

"Whatcha reading?"

"Our favorite fashion bible from when we were in high school, because, Lord knows, they need my money while my self-esteem is at its lowest, and I'm actually old enough to actually relate to the advice articles. It had this article about different ways to handle heartbreak, and I gotta say that it's a bit different from anything they have published in the past. Like this one—'*M* is for Me Time' is such a roller-coaster ride I don't know if I should sue them for whiplash or applaud them for hitting it head on. *M* is for me time because, of course, it is!" Stacey began to read the article.

> DO: Make sure you are getting back to your own roots and doing what you love to do. Remember that you love walking along the river, and your ex wanted to walk through their Xbox achievements? Do it! It'll give you some fresh air, some endorphins running through you, and a chance to see just how strong and independent you are. DON'T: Revert into yourself. Stewing over those "I could have done things differently" or "I should have seen the signs" scenarios

isn't healthy, and you are at your best when you're healthy.

Stacey finished strong with a mocking tone.

Mary let out a long and low whistle. "That's some heavy shit; you're right about that. But I have to applaud them for using inclusive language," she said.

"What do you mean?"

"Instead of saying things like 'his Xbox,' they said 'their Xbox.' I'm surprised they had it in them." Mary gestured with a piece of toast toward the magazine and took a long drink.

Stacey followed suit before she mentioned her suspicion that the magazine might have a new writer.

"Now I need to read the rest of the article to see what other kind of inclusive language they used," Mary said with her expectant hand out toward the magazine.

"Honestly, it's just a bunch of love-yourself blurbs and *Legally Blonde* references," Stacey said as she passed it over.

"So what had you so focused on it then?"

"Probably the list in general and the one actually about lists. I feel like it would really help me. But I have absolutely no idea what kind of list to make besides different ways I can vandalize Tyler's belongings, and that's frowned upon in this establishment."

A few awkward moments passed between the two of them as they both internally lobbied back and forth with different ideas, gaping their mouths a couple of times when they thought they had an idea, but dismissing it before they could make a sound.

"Dream vacations?" Mary suggested.

"Too cliché. Besides, I really wouldn't be able to go on any of them because they would require a passport and Duolingo's green-owl mascot harassing me every other hour. Maybe I could go with US cities I'd want to visit?"

"God, I feel that's worse. What's something you want to work on?"

Mary tipped back her bottle and walked back toward the fridge. "You want another one?" she asked as she opened another for herself.

Stacey could feel the start of a familiar tingling through her fingers, but she wasn't feeling anything anywhere else. "Sure and, honestly, I want to work on roller skating, but that would make for a very short list."

"Short list! That's it!" Mary exclaimed with a slap to her thigh.

Stacey gave her a concerned once-over and dramatically leaned away from her. "I don't know if I'm going to like where this is going."

"You said you wished you had more experience with guys. I think you should make a list of guys you wanna bang."

"The only flaw with that is I don't think Adam Driver, Michael B. Jordan, or that gloriously tall East Asian from *13 Reasons Why* would be that easily accessible or enough to mark them off of the list."

"Listen here, smart-ass. You'll have to make it a bit more realistic. But how?"

They both gave their bottles a tip back, and when Stacey looked back down at the article, it felt as if an actual light bulb went off in her head; she almost spit some cider out. "I hit all the letters in the alphabet!" she exclaimed. She drew in a deep breath before she continued, "So that's a total of nineteen guys I need to bang." Stacey said sadly, "Oh God, that's really high. Would I even be able to attract that many guys?" She started to think of all the possible flaws that would keep potential guys from coming around.

Mary saw where Stacey's mind was headed, and she gave her friend's knee a quick shake to bring her back to Earth. "Hey, remember letter *M*? Stay with me here, bitch. I know you have a DNR somewhere."

"Sorry, it's just…it was hard for me to get the guys that I got before, so how am I going to get anywhere close to the full alphabet before I die?"

"You have to stop being so fucking hard on yourself. You're a strong, bad bitch who's going somewhere in life, which is definitely a lot more than can be said about Tyler and his shitty personality, and even worse work ethic."

"I guess you're right," Stacey said, not wanting to get into another round of obligatory esteem boosters with Mary because, of course, she, as a best friend, would say all those things.

"Damn right, I'm right. Now, let's get this list up and going so we can get this tit show on the road."

"Don't you mean shit show?" Stacey asked.

"I know what I'm about," Mary said as she started rummaging through the drawers in the entertainment center for construction paper and colored pencils.

* * *

An hour later, a sticker-covered sheet of construction paper lay in front of them; they had started the list—Stacey's very own ABCs of Heartbreak. It may have taken a few tears, another couple rounds of drinks, and one or two paper cuts, but they were proud of what they had made.

Stacey pushed out a long sigh of relief, but it was stopped short when she saw how many empty spaces there were. A few more tears threatened to escape, but she blinked them away when Mary clapped her hands once in satisfaction.

"It's a masterpiece, if I do say so myself," Mary said.

"Where do I even begin? I feel like it's going to be even harder to go alphabetically than the thought of even doing this."

"Just go through it when you can. It's your list; take charge of it, and get to it. But I know just the thing that will help you get started."

"I swear to God, if you say Tinder, I'm going to throat punch you."

"We'll just have to sign you up for that one dating app with the flame as the logo," Mary said.

Stacey let out a groan at being bested, flopped onto her back on the floor, and splayed her arms out to the sides dramatically.

CHAPTER
5

"You ready?" Mary asked as she looked over at Stacey's pale face. They stood at the front steps of what was no longer Stacey and Tyler's apartment building, mentally preparing themselves. They'd arrived in a U-Haul van with a half-dozen cardboard boxes and plastic tote bins at the ready in the back.

Stacey looked at the front door and then up to the third floor to see the light-green curtains, which she had purchased, fluttering in the breeze of the AC. Her breathing alternated between marching in double time to almost stopping altogether. Mary gave her a soft tap on the shoulder; the low rush running through Stacey's ears dissipated, and all her surroundings came into focus all at once.

"You ready to tear this place apart? We've got four hours before he gets back from work. You have the key, right?"

Stacey pulled the key chain out of her back pocket and gave it a little shake for jangling proof. They entered the building and proceeded up to the apartment. Stacey chose a key from the ring, inserted it into the keyhole, turned the lock of the apartment door, and braced herself before opening the door.

After just two weeks, it felt like a completely new place. The picture frames had changed, as had anything that held *their* memories. All the different knickknacks in and on the bookshelf by the door, the container in which they kept their keys—they were all gone. She glanced around and realized that even a couple of bookcases were missing.

She walked through the living room, trying hard not to focus on the throw blanket on the couch—it wasn't hers—and into the bedroom. Stacey noticed the smell first. It no longer smelled like her sweet and floral perfume but instead of *her* musky yet sweet vanilla-like smell. The bed was unmade, which was something she had taken pride in doing every morning when she was with Tyler, and the pillowcases had been changed.

It wasn't until she saw a thriller novel on the nightstand on *her* side of the bed that it hit Stacey with full force that *she* had completely made herself at home here, had completely taken her place…and *she* was so different from Stacey.

"How you doing?" Mary asked suddenly from behind her, causing Stacey to jump a little.

Stacey clutched her imaginary pearls to soothe her racing heart before turning around to face Mary. "Take it all," was all she said.

Mary looked from side to side, and her eyes held one big question. "What exactly is 'all'?"

"Anything that I paid for. Those green curtains in the living room, the silverware, a few of the pots and pans in the cupboard...three different bookcases, even though I don't know where they are."

"I think he may have started that and left them in the spare bedroom. There were some bookshelves and piles of books in one of the corners."

The thought that Tyler had already started packing up her stuff was a punch to the gut, but Stacey squared her shoulders and kept her head high as she made a lap around the apartment, taking inventory of different things.

"Hello?" They heard from the front door when they were in the bathroom.

"In here, Krista!" Mary yelled.

Krista came around the corner. After one look at Stacey's face, she wrapped her up in the tightest hug she could muster.

The three of them soon had a good system going: Krista and Mary helped lug things down to the truck while Stacey packed up everything that she could.

They had gone through the bathroom and the spare bedroom after an hour and had made it to the master bedroom. Stacey opened up the closet and looked at all her clothes that still hung on her side. She stuffed them into garbage bags, garment-bag style, and looked over at his clothes on their hangers. Without a second's hesitation, she pulled the shirts and pants of his that were on hangers she paid for and simply left them on the floor in front of the closet doors. She was putting the last one in another garbage bag when Mary walked in.

She looked between Stacey and the clothes lying on the floor. "Oh, so when you said all, you really meant *all*. I'm in. What else is there?"

"That lamp by the door. Now they will have to walk all the way to the side of the bed for lighting at night."

"Fuck yeah. Is there anything else I can do to make things inconvenient for them?" Mary said with a devilish rub of her palms.

Krista walked in, sweat dripping down her temples. "It is as hot as a mother out there. I think we might have to make two trips if there's any more big things," she said as she eyed the four garbage bags at Stacey's feet.

"This might be the biggest. All we have left is the kitchen; then we should be good to go."

"That should fit perfectly then," Krista said. Mary and she grabbed the bags, two each, and took them down to the truck.

Stacey looked around, and her eyes landed on Tyler's underwear drawer; inspiration struck. She grabbed all his boxers and tossed them onto the floor of the closet in the spare room, making sure to close the closet door behind her. She made her way back to the bathroom and took the shower liner off the rings, leaving them on the bar, which she left in the tub. She was on her way to the kitchen when Mary and Krista came back in.

"So what are we taking next?" Mary asked.

"The laundry detergent in the linen closet, but not the fabric-softener sheets. Other than that, it's nothing but pots and pans and silverware in the kitchen; we should be good from there."

Mary sagged in disappointment. "But I wanted to fuck something else up."

Krista looked around the room, and her eyes landed on the two power strips on the floor below the TV. "What if we unplugged everything in the living room?" Krista suggested.

"This is why I love you. But why stop at the living room? Why not unplug everything in the apartment?"

"I draw the line at the fridge," Stacey chimed in.

"Gotta have limits at some point, I guess."

It was another two hours before they all crashed on various soft surfaces in Mary's living room. Krista opted for the throw rug, pressing her cheek to the hardwood floor just over the edge of it, while Mary laid claim to the couch; Stacey, the armchair.

"I really do appreciate you two; I hope you know that," Stacey said after the flush from the heat had cooled from her cheeks and shoulders.

They grunted and gave Stacey a half-assed salute in unison.

* * *

Later that night, after they took turns taking rapid showers to make sure there was enough hot water for everyone, Krista, Mary, and Stacey sat crunched together on the couch. Stacey sat in the middle while Krista and Mary expectantly looked over each of her shoulders as they eagerly waited for the download wheel of the app to complete its cycle.

"It's like trying to boil a pot of water. Does it know we are watching it or something?" Mary whined.

Stacey and Krista rolled their eyes in unison, and they completely missed the app popping up. Mary reached out and tapped Stacey's screen to get her attention. Stacey flinched defensively away from her.

Mary brought up her hands in surrender. "If you guys weren't being Debbie Downers, you would have seen it too."

Stacey rolled her eyes and glanced down at the cheerful "Welcome" that flashed back at her. After a cleansing breath, Stacey skipped through the obligatory tutorial pages of the dating app and finally landed on the page to start uploading pictures.

"Do you know what pictures you want to use? If not, I suggest that one beach picture of yours from last year. The one with the glare of the sunset silhouetting you?" Mary said.

Stacey froze for a second in a momentary bout of panic as she tried to recall some of her best pictures and came up blank.

Mary misinterpreted Stacey's hesitation and kept explaining the exact day the picture was taken.

"No, I remember the picture. I was just trying to remember some other good ones."

"Do you not have a folder in your Camera Roll for just such an occasion?" Mary asked.

Krista leaned forward to look at Mary and shared the same baffled look as Stacey had.

"What? How do you think I cycled through so many profiles? I had to keep it updated. And I never would have met you if I hadn't," Mary said as she jutted her chin in Krista's direction.

"I guess I am more unprepared than I thought I would be." Stacey sighed, ending the exhale with a hint of sarcasm.

"How about this? Let's at least start with the beach one, and if you stumble across another good one on your way through the Camera Roll, you can add it. If not, we can go back with fresh eyes after the prompts," Krista suggested.

A bottle of wine, a heated debate on the best angles for a selfie and for a group photo, and a final selection of four pictures later, they had found a perfect photo for each aspect Stacey was trying to feature: a group picture to show she had friends, a picture of Mary and Stacey on a pedal boat to show she was fun, one from when she was younger and an active volunteer at a local pet shelter to show she was good with animals, and a full-body picture because, as Mary mused, "Apparently that matters to straight dudes."

The very next page instructed her to answer questions that ranged from views on unpopular opinions, to favorite ways to spend a Sunday and about what she was most competitive. Stacey started skipping through the prompts faster and faster as she realized she had nothing funny or interesting to add.

"Let's just pick a random one for now. Close your eyes, and swipe until I say stop," Mary instructed.

Stacey dramatically slapped one hand over her eyes, and the other began swiping away after she uttered the smallest "ow."

"And stop!"

Stacey looked down and read, "Two truths and a lie," on the screen. "Well, shit," she mumbled.

"Think of a blatant lie, and go from there," Krista said.

Without thinking, Stacey immediately answered, "That my favorite season is winter."

"Perfect. Now just think of a couple of good truths, but let them be conversation pieces."

"Don't know how many things that have happened to me that guys would consider to be conversation pieces, but let me think for a minute." As an agonizing, over-the-atrical rendition of the "Final Jeopardy" theme was sung by both Krista and Mary, a thought popped into Stacey's head. "That time at the mall with Alice Cooper!"

"What? With the where?" Krista asked, taken aback by the sudden outburst.

"When I was in high school, I was at the mall, in a Hot Topic, and the salespeople were hovering around a couple of older men; one looked oddly familiar. When they got out one of their phones to take a picture, I realized it was Alice Cooper. Alice Cooper was in the same Hot Topic as I was, and at one point was only three feet away from me"

"What did you do afterward?"

"I panicked and walked out of the store without buying anything."

"Yeah, that sounds like you." Mary chuckled.

"But that still leaves one more truth. Make it a stupid one where the guys will almost fight you about it," Krista said.

Stacey scrunched up her face and made a confused look. "I don't know if I'd want to be fighting these boys that early in a relationship."

"No, like one of the ones where they will get defensive for like no reason and think you're not a person because of it. Like butter instead of cream cheese on a bagel."

"Or like saying it's pronounced 'soda' around people that call it 'pop.' I've had my fair share of heated conversations about that."

"Exactly like that, but not that one. That one feels politically charged, and it's not a vibe," Mary said.

"Noted. How about that I've never owned a dog before."

Both Krista and Mary hesitated for a second before agreeing that it would be a good one to use.

"Just keep your guard up if you match with someone who has a dog. They are like missionaries in a country they don't belong in. Spoiler alert: it's all of them," Krista said.

Flabbergasted, Stacey's jaw dropped for a moment before Krista snapped her fingers a few times. They cycled through the prompts three times before they settled on "I will never get over…" and "I recently learned…"

"I hate how much it feels like a Broadway production, and I'm the lead, the pit, and the backstage crew all at once." Stacey groaned as she slumped into the couch.

"But that's the thing with online dating—you need to make a good first impression because of how quickly you're judged," Mary mused from her relocated spot on the floor. For added flair, she looked down her nose as she watched the Pinot Grigio twirl in her wineglass.

"If you say so."

"And don't go immediately swiping left because a guy's first picture isn't good. They don't always have the best sense when it comes to this, so give them the benefit of the doubt," Krista piped in.

Willfully ignoring that blatant red flag of a double standard, Stacey took a grounding breath before she started swiping.

"Shit, a fish picture right off the bat," Mary said as Stacey presented her phone, YouTube makeup-artist style, to the other two women.

"Yeah, but the next one is of him and his grandmother. Redemption," Krista added.

"So what are his prompts?"

Stacey listed, "That he is competitive about everything, a two-truths, one-lie prompt, and that he became a family lawyer because of what he went through when he was younger. Kinda heavy, but definitely a badge of honor, I would say."

Krista and Mary literally scratched their chins as they thought for a moment. "Swipe right," Mary said just as Krista asked, "What are the truths and lie?" Mary gave Krista a look of betrayal, and Krista just shrugged her shoulders in response.

"That he's a twin, he studied abroad in Italy, and he's completely color blind."

"Yeah, that's a right swipe. They aren't crass, and they all actually have some thought behind them. Regardless of what the truths are, they are good conversation pieces. Seven out of ten."

They kept at the peanut-gallery style voting process for another couple of hours and bottles of wine.

CHAPTER
6

"For the love of…it isn't even 6:00 a.m.," Stacey groaned as she rolled onto her other side and blindly reached over to the coffee table for her phone the following Monday morning. As a third message pinged on her phone, she was finally able to flick the switch into vibration mode.

"This is why they have that little switch on the side, ya know!" Mary yelled groggily from her bedroom.

"Better late than never," Stacey mumbled back. She rubbed her eyes, instantly regretting that decision when she felt the grit of her mascara as it built up on her finger with each swipe.

She cracked open one of her eyes and saw that she had three notifications from Tinder, all from a guy named Brad. Before she could open her phone to view them, the alarm went off. "It's 6:00 a.m. Couldn't he have waited another minute?" she grumbled to herself out loud.

Brad: *Hey there sexy ;)*

Brad: *I actualy hav a important question for u*

Brad: *Do u like pineapple on pizza?*

Stacey stared at the screen for a long moment while she tried to process what was shot at her at six in the morning. After she rubbed her face, thinking it would help form a reply, she gave it a try.

Stacey: *Hey cutie. I don't actually *smiling sweat-drop emoji* but i am a pretty big fan of meat lovers ;)*

She hit Send and immediately felt dirty for being so cheesy. "If this is what it's always going to be like on this app, I'm getting five cats," she yelled to Mary. All she heard in reply was someone rolling over and feet hitting the floor.

"You'd be getting an eviction notice from me real quick."

"Meanie. You would do that to your best friend?"

"Hell yeah, I only like one type of kitty cat, and it comes between two legs."

"God, it's too early for all of this horny shit. This guy started off this conversation with a 'hey, sexy.'"

"Let me get my coffee first; then we can drag his ass."

Stacey took a sip of her peppermint-mocha-flavored coffee and let the warmth gloriously trail down her throat before handing her phone to Mary.

"He's trying way too hard. But I have to admit that is a pretty crafty pickup line. Everyone has an opinion on pineapple on pizza, and most people always want to share it."

"I was honestly half tempted to go with the full-on disgusted route, but thought better of it."

"Good, you don't need to be pulling out the crazy that early."

They went back and forth with different ways to handle guys who were too forward, who were slow repliers, and who would turn if they didn't receive a reply fast enough.

"Men suck," Stacey said after Mary showed her examples of men who became aggressive after women didn't reply to their toolish messages.

"Why do you think I play for the other team?" Mary joked.

A twitter notification buzzed through on Stacey's phone, and she looked to see that it was already 7:00 a.m. "Shit, we gotta get ready for work. I am *not* about to use a taxi to get to work. I'm sure it would be faster to walk."

* * *

"Mmkay, so can anyone give me a rundown of the notes from last week's meeting?" Steve asked as the last couple of people squeezed into the conference room just before he closed the door on them. "That would be great." He looked at the tittering interns as they disappointedly stood in the corners of the room.

Stacey swore she saw a hint of an eye roll from the sixty-something-year-old, and she had to cough into her hand to hide the surprised laugh that suddenly bubbled up.

"Did he just—" Greg whispered to her.

All Stacey could do to keep from laughing out loud was to give him an enthusiastic nod.

"Stacey, would you like to give the highlights of last week's meeting, seeing as you are so excited to be here today?" Steve said.

A hush fell over the room, and Stacey boiled with a blush. It had been a while since she had been chastised like a schoolgirl, and she had a bachelor's to prove just how long ago it was. "I guess I could," she replied.

"Our May issue was a hit with its focus on mothers and different do-it-yourselfs that could include the kids. There was some backlash in regards to the language; some comments on social media deemed the article condescending because of the simplistic ideas that 'seemed to have been dumbed down so women could understand.' So that means Henry isn't allowed to write any more articles that focus on women," Stacey said.

There were a few snickers throughout the room, and Steve waved his hand in an impatient keep-it-moving motion.

"There was a suggestion last week for an article focused on easy fix hacks for the dad with a long honey-do list. We put Steph, Daisy, and Mike in charge of research for the article, and Steph will handle properly citing any and all of the sites and sources used. We will also need to look into the structure of houses in, I think, South Dakota for the 'Travel the 50 States' feature piece.

"I think that's it, Steve," Stacey finished.

Steve gave her a quick nod and started talking about new topics to include in the next issue.

Stacey leaned back in her chair and started to zone out while focusing on a little bit of writing that was missed on the whiteboard the last time it was wiped clean. She snapped back to Earth when she felt a light tapping on her arm, tuning back in to find Greg had leaned in close so he could whisper in her ear.

"Your phone keeps going off. Good thing you have it on vibrate, or else Steve would have scolded you like a ten-year-old again. When did you become Miss Popular?" he asked.

She looked down to see there were three different men messaging her on Tinder. She placed her phone screen side down on her lap. "I get notifications when people I follow on Twitter tweet anything new, and sometimes it can get a bit overwhelming."

"I didn't realize Twitter added a winking emoji whenever someone liked you—I mean, tweeted you."

She saw that damned-cocky half smile wash over his face as if he were the cat that ate the canary. Her jaw dropped, but she snapped it back up before she caught any flies. The butterflies in her stomach kicked back up again, and she quickly looked away from Greg.

Just as quickly, the sly smile slipped from his face, and his mouth dipped into a scowl as he stared at the back of her head.

"Must be an update you don't have yet," she said softly over her shoulder.

"So exclusive. Maybe you can let me in on the secret soon?"

She glanced back for a quick moment and was only able to focus on him locking his eyes with hers and winking. She started blushing so hard she was sure she was going to have a bloody nose.

"Shh, I wanna know what kind of misogynistic article he wants us to write this month," Stacey said.

Greg quietly coughed up a short laugh and pretended to clear his throat when a few of the heads closest to them turned their way.

"Does anyone have any questions?" Steve said.

Stacey snapped her head toward him and realized she hadn't heard a word he said.

Everyone avoided eye contact with Steve to get the meeting to finish as soon as possible.

"Shit, what did I miss?" she asked Lisa as soon as they made it back to their cubicles.

"If you hadn't been flirting with Greg, you would have heard that there really wasn't anything said," she shot back.

"We weren't flirting. He was just warning me about my cell phone being on the table."

"I'm sure. Why would you be worried about your phone anyway?"

"Because her Tinder was blowing up," Greg said over his divider.

Stacey picked up an almost-disapproving tone from him, but she shook it off and just shot him an icy glare.

"It's only been—what?—two weeks since the breakup, and you are on Tinder already?"

"It was my friend Mary's idea."

"Sure it was. When you're ready to admit that you aren't as heartbroken as you lead people to believe, I'll be here waiting." Lisa spun in her chair and faced her screens.

Stacey flipped her off, just out of the range of Lisa's peripheral vision. Much to her delight, Greg saw it and gave her an approving nod. Their eyes held for a couple of moments, and Stacey had to spin around in her own chair to tamp down the desire to jump over the desks to slap him or kiss him. And she was worried that she wasn't certain which of the two options she wanted to feel more.

* * *

So where would your dream vacation be? Stacey messaged back to one of the three Erics who'd matched with her. Her very first reaction had been to worry she would mix one up with the others, but each one was worse than the last, and one only lasted three exchanges.

Sorry, not sorry, that I'm not interested in a threesome with your girlfriend, she thought when she blocked one of them.

I haven't done much traveling but I think I would want to go visit Greece or something to see where my grandfather came from, Eric 2 replied within moments.

She was impressed that he went immediately to a culture-based vacation, which was a pleasant relief from all the very unintelligent interactions she had had so far.

Greece seems like such a beautiful country, especially some of the smaller hillside towns that overlook the sea, she responded and then messaged back and forth with him about other locations they would want to visit, but then it seemed to come to a standstill. In a panic, she messaged him a quick excuse, *I'm working late tonight so I'll message you when I get out?*

He replied with a simple affirmative, and she rested her head on her desk. The office was quiet, even at just 5:10 p.m., and she relished the reprieve.

"You haven't left either? Too busy messaging all those people on Twitter?" Greg said out of nowhere with a very obvious tone of derision.

Stacey startled in her chair because she hadn't realized he was still there, but she never lifted her head to glare at him. *He probably made air quotes,* she thought.

"Just another busy day for social-justice warriors like me."

"Would a social-justice warrior be up for a drink?" Greg asked.

He sounded closer, so she turned her face away from the sound of his voice. Her breathing started to pick up without her consent, and she tried to count to five before attempting a coherent answer. Finally, she managed to get out, "Maybe not tonight. Some other time?"

"That sounds good. Let me know, will ya? Have a good night."

She listened to his footsteps fade and waited until she couldn't hear them anymore before she released the breath she, until that moment, hadn't realized she was holding.

Get ahold of yourself already, Stacey thought to herself. She took one more deep and refreshing breath before she got up and grabbed her purse. Her phone went off once more, and she looked down to see a message from Brad.

So when am I going to get a taste of that pussy?

She laughed out loud at the sudden and explicit message he'd sent out of the blue. Sure, they had been messaging back and forth throughout the day, gradually getting a little more dirty each time, but this sudden attempt to grab her attention humored her more than anything. She took a screenshot of it and started for the elevators.

* * *

"He said what?" Mary asked as she sat at the kitchen table.

Stacey pulled the frozen pizza out of the oven and sat down across from her while she waited for it to cool. "I have the screenshot to prove it. I honestly laughed when I got it." She passed her phone over, and Mary almost fell out of her chair as she laughed.

"Yo, that is too good. I feel like, in all actuality, he had an average or smaller-than-average dick, and this over-selling of his sexual prowess is his way of masking it. I bet you are eating up some of the other shit he has been writing you though, right?"

Stacey had to think about it, but she soon realized that just the mention of what he would do to her made her want to believe he actually would. Thinking about that left her in so intense a heated anticipation that she had to relieve herself in the shower when she got home from work.

"Will you believe me if I said no?"

"No. So I feel like you might just have to bite the bullet and hook up with him to see if he really is more than just talk. Plus, he's a letter that you need to add to the list."

Mary got up and started cutting into the pizza. She took a bite and instantly regretted it. "Shit, why didn't you warn me?"

"Maybe because you saw me pull it out of the oven not even two minutes ago?"

"That's cold," Mary mumbled through another bite.

"Unlike that pizza," Stacey countered.

Mary took another bite, and her eyes started to water. But she continued to chew, and stared down Stacey as she did.

"I get it; you're the main bitch. We all knew this; my period has been in sync with yours for the past year."

"Damn straight. Ooh, what did he say?" Mary asked when she saw Stacey's phone light up.

Stacey read, "*I'm gonna pound that pussy so hard. Will you be screaming my name while I do it?* And then he did the semicolon-parenthesis smiling wink."

"Jesus, where the fuck did this kid get his material? I've seen better material from the people on *My 600-lb Life*," Mary grumbled.

Stacey took a deep breath and tried not to laugh, but failed.

I def will be, if I can catch my breath enough from moaning, Mary wrote in reply for Stacey.

"That's worse than what he sent!" Stacey gasped.

"You'll thank me later."

* * *

As she walked up the stairs to the second floor of the five-story walk-up, Stacey realized Mary was right; Brad had taken the very forward bait and had asked for her to come over that Friday.

A door opened down the hall to the left, and a man popped out. He looked exactly like the picture on his profile—tall, dusty-blond hair, five-o'clock shadow, long jaw, and fun yet goofy grin. He gave her an approving smile after his once-over. "Hey, come on in," he said.

Stacey stepped in and was immediately confused about where she was. She looked to her left and saw a modern-style love seat, a cream-colored shag throw blanket, and flower-shaped coasters on the table. She looked to her right and saw the dining room table with a fabric tablecloth and a random cluster of fake flowers in a small vase in the middle.

"Where should I take my shoes off?" Stacey asked to break the awkwardness that she felt had grown between them.

"Right next to the door is fine—"

Before he could finish his sentence, she heard banging and a loud moan from the room farthest away. Stacey froze in place.

Brad chuckled when he saw her look of fear and confusion. "It's my roommate; she has someone over right now. Hope you don't mind. She's always so loud; it just turns me on and makes me so hard. Like right now," he said while his hand hovered over his pants.

He stepped over to her in one step and crushed his lips to hers. His urgency, the dominating of her lips, and the way his hand gripped her hair made her almost forget about the moaning woman in the room twenty feet from her. His other hand found the hem of her shirt, and his fingers grazed the heated skin of her hips and stomach.

She pulled away from the kiss, in fear of taking her shirt off, but the fevered look in his eyes melted her shirt off for her. She unbuckled his belt and tried to unbutton his pants, but a loud bang threw her off-balance.

"Get me out of here," Brad moaned as he pulled down his pants in one swift move. His rock-hard cock reached toward her; it was actually a little bigger than Stacey expected, and she made a mental note to prove Mary wrong when she got home.

He stroked his dick a couple of times right there in the foyer, and Stacey grew more worried by the second. "Shouldn't we go to the bedroom?"

"We can, but we won't be caught if we fool around a little bit out here first."

He held her in a kiss once more and pushed her up against the door. One hand trailed down to her pants, and he, after a couple of attempts, was able to undo them. He reached down and, using the friction of her panties, started to rub her clit, or at least where he thought her clit would be.

She mentally applauded his brazen nature and moaned against his lips.

He pulled away, smiled down at her, and moaned something unintelligible. He grabbed her hand and walked her to the bedroom next to the one with the moaning woman.

Stacey looked around and quickly realized that the head of his bed was up against the dividing wall between the two bedrooms.

But before she could think any further about it, Brad pushed her onto the bed and pulled her pants off. He crawled on top of her, and while he had her pinned under his thighs, he rolled on a condom.

"I can't wait to be inside you."

"I can't wait either. Oh God, I'm so hot right now."

CHAPTER
7

"'Oh God, I'm so hot right now'? You really need to work on your sexy talk," Mary commented.

They'd stopped for coffee after their spin class the following morning because Stacey had made spilling her story an incentive for Mary to push harder during the class.

"He was into it, so I figured it wouldn't hurt to just say something," she said with an Anna Faris-type shoulder shrug. "You know they were still going at it when we finished? I don't know if that says something about how long they could go, or about how short it was with Brad. But I'm being honest when I say it was him. Oh, and he was a little bigger than I was expecting."

"You feel so happy to prove me wrong, don't you?" Mary sneered.

Stacey just gave her a proud nod of the head and then took a sip of her coffee to signal she'd had the final word.

Mary simply gave her a shake of her head, but was stopped short when Stacey's phone lit up to signal a message had come in from Eric 2. "It's been five days with this guy! Have you hooked up with him yet?"

"No, we haven't. He has a really weird schedule, and I feel like he is actually the most mature out of all of the ones I've talked to so far."

"Oh? How so?"

"I mean, he talks about wanting to get to know his family roots; he's crazy serious about his family; he's goal-oriented and is very good at his career. Oh, and he has a daughter." Stacey finished in a rush to make sure that last bit of news timed perfectly with Mary taking a sip.

Just as she had hoped, Mary spit a little back into her cup and coughed to help her breathing get back to normal. "How is that not the very first thing you would bring up? A daughter? How old?"

"Two, and she's the cutest little nugget. But I don't think he knows how to wipe her face because there is always something around her mouth or caked under her nose in the pictures he's sent me of her."

"He must be serious if he is showing off his dirty daughter."

"I guess so. I want to get to know him more, to see if he truly is as much of a gentleman as he claims to be."

"Besides the kid, there has to be something else wrong with him."

"Besides the fact that his baby mama had kids from other guys? I can't think of anything."

At that, Mary had to push her coffee cup completely away. She brought her hands up to her mouth and looked Stacey over. "You need to cut your losses because nothing good will come from baby-mama drama."

"But I can't just ghost him! He's been so nice to me."

"We'll figure it out soon enough. But we gotta go because this coffee is doing some bad things to me right now."

* * *

Eric 2: *You're going to get me in trouble at work if you keep talking like tha*t

Stacey lay on the couch, hair still wet from the shower, with her phone hovering above her. A small smile crept over her face as she thought of how just a couple of words that simply hinted at something sexual could excite such a gentleman. *That must be what gentlemen are actually like, still refined but ready to show you a good time,* she thought to herself.

Wouldn't want to do that, but I do have to admit some of the thoughts running through my mind aren't work appropriate ;), she replied. A little part of her actually was thinking of some Fabio-cover scenarios, and she willed her mind to only go as far as the camera flash.

Trust me, the things I'm thinking of doing to you, simply by staring into your deep-brown eyes, is making me hate work right now

She blushed and a thrilling chill ran down her spine as her mind continued to wander.

Maybe we can talk more about this when you're on break?

If we do, you'll make me do worse things than a celibate monk

It took her a moment to think of the meaning of that message, and once she did, she audibly exclaimed a simple "Oh shit!"

"What did you do this time?" Mary yelled from her room.

"I didn't do anything, but Eric 2 is getting hot and bothered at work."

"Whatcha guys talking about?"

Mary wandered out of her room with a small shoebox in hand, and when she passed Stacey to sit in the armchair, the intense smell of acetone and nail polish hit her in the face. Meanwhile, Stacey's hands momentarily forgot how to hold a phone, and it landed corner down on her lip.

"Fuck," she muttered. She sat up in an embarrassed huff and safely placed her phone on the coffee table.

"'Fucking' is the correct tense of that verb. You of all people should know that, Ms. English Degree," Mary said while she dramatically looked between two colors of nail polish, holding one up at a time as if her hands were a set of scales. "Purple," she finally uttered.

"I really hate you sometimes. No, we were talking in a very PG-13 manner, and he sent me this," Stacey said as she unlocked her phone to show Mary.

Mary looked up and slightly cocked her head in a "You're kidding me, right?" look.

Stacey just shrugged and started to smile when she saw another message from Eric 2 pop up.

*I had to look that up just to make sure I was using it correctly *smiling sweat-drop emoji**

Stacey couldn't help the nose exhale that bubbled out of her. "Jesus, he's so cute. He said he had to look it up to make sure he was using it correctly."

"Which means he's trying. Maybe you'll be cutting that list out soon if he keeps this up."

Stacey couldn't decipher what level of sarcasm Mary had used with that retort, but she assumed very little when she realized Mary's attention was actually on using her left hand to paint the nails on her right.

It was well worth it because it was really funny. And if I'm being honest, you make me want to say some very unladylike things

Oh? Like what? ;)

Like describing some things I would do to you

No one else is here right now so you can say whatever you want to me

In that case, I can't wait for you to take control of me, after I've ridden you of course ;)

"You need another shower? A cold one this time?" Mary said.

Stacey snapped out of her heated stupor and realized she had been biting her lip and breathing a little faster than normal.

"If he's doing this to you now, just imagine what he would do to you in person."

"And that kind of thought really will drive me to take a cold shower." Stacey fanned herself with her hand and pretended to faint in a way that would make Scarlett O'Hara proud.

Her phone buzzed once more, and she quickly grabbed it, anxious to see what Eric 2 had to say in reply. Instead, she saw a message from a man named Peter, who started off his message with a standard "Hey there, sexy" variation.

"And then there's this asshole," she said. She opened the app to view his profile and realized that he was way out of her league. She swiped through his pictures: one shirtless to show off his six-pack, one close-up to showcase his square jaw, perfect teeth, and the smallest hint of a dimple on his left cheek.

"Jesus, how did he match with me?" Stacey asked frantically as she shoved her phone in Mary's face.

"I mean, I guess I see it, but he's not my type. Besides, you're a beautiful woman who happens to have some nice curves. It was bound to happen."

"You guess? Fuck, he looks like Captain America!" Stacey continued to ponder and question what exactly had made him swipe right on her.

Hey ;) how are ya? she sent.

Just chillin. Wishing I had someone to chill with ;)

Stacey gaped at his response and clicked on her own profile to see what pictures she had posted of herself. One full-mirror selfie, check. Two headshots to showcase her ability to make bedroom eyes, check. One with Mary to make it seem as if she actually does have friends, check. She couldn't piece together exactly what he was seeing, but she decided to indulge him, and herself, so she responded, *Great minds think alike, I guess.*

You available tonight? he quickly messaged back.

I can be ;)

Good. Send me some pics?

Stacey was stunned for a moment at how quickly he was going. It took her a moment to remember the standard bra and thong pictures that took her forever to take because of the awkward angle she had to hold the phone over her shoulder. She sent them both off with a moment's hesitation and tagged them with a request for some from him.

Damn you're so hot. Ur making me so hard right now

I want to suck that huge cock so bad

Come and get it then ;)

Stacey flushed with both nervousness and anticipation, all at the same time, and could barely get any words out to Mary.

"Did someone die?" Mary asked after she noticed how flustered Stacey had suddenly become.

"I don't know if he is being honest or not, but he wants to hook up, like, right now. After messaging me for like five minutes."

"That's the beauty of Tinder, honey. That's one of the better parts of it. Unless he gets creepily attached afterward —then that's the other side of Tinder, which is very scary."

"I know. I've heard the stories. I'm mostly just confused. Of all the people he could be hooking up with, he's messaging me to hook up?"

"Girl, how many times do I have to tell you? You're hot. Now go get that subpar dick and check it off your list."

* * *

Thirty-five minutes later, Stacey walked up to a condo that was a little farther away from her than the app claimed it was. Only one light was on in the condo, and she had to message Peter to make sure she was at the correct address. A moment later, a tall figure popped his head out of the door, and even in the poor lighting from the street lamps, she could see his smile, which was just like the one in the picture.

"You made it," he said.

She walked up the steps and followed him inside. "I thought I passed it because they all tend to look the same."

"I had the same problem when I first moved in. For a full month, I kept going up to the neighbor's door and was so confused when my key wouldn't work," he said. He raised his arm and scratched the back of his head, and Stacey could see that he had very well-defined arms; she also spotted the line of a defined hip below his abs.

"Let's head upstairs." He led her upstairs and into the second room to the right.

His room was sparse, and she couldn't get an idea of who he was. After she spotted six different containers of protein powder and post-workout whatever, she had her answer. She mentally shrugged, took her jacket off, and placed it on the computer chair, which was missing a desk, next to the bed.

"What kind of movies do you like?" he asked, remote in hand, as he nervously alternated between Hulu and Netflix on the Roku home screen.

"Different types, and I honestly spend more time going through Netflix than actually watching something."

"I have the same problem!" he said. He clicked on Netflix and turned back to Stacey while the app loaded. "It doesn't help that they keep adding movies and TV shows, which I will admit are pretty good."

"I said that to a coworker the other day when he was telling me about a new show they just added."

"Anything good?"

"It wasn't something I would have been into, so the conversation ended real quick," Stacey said with a shrug.

Peter gave a slow, understanding nod, and he finally ended up putting on *The Office*.

"Good choice."

"Oh, I'm not a fan of it; I won't get distracted by it. You can sit on the bed if you'd like," he said as he watched her sway from foot to foot.

Once she was on the bed, he lay down next to her and propped himself up on one of his elbows. "So you're a fan of this show?"

"Yeah, I like it because it's simple. It's one of those shows that you can put on in the background while doing things around the house or something, and you won't really feel like you missed anything. Which is good. But some of the jokes are written off the cuff sometimes; you do need to be watching to catch all of them."

"Maybe I'll have to give this show a chance then."

"The first couple of episodes are hard to get through, but that's just the writers trying to get across the basis of the show and all of its characters," Stacey said.

She looked down at Peter and found him staring up at her. She searched his face to see if she could get an idea of what he was thinking, but he answered her by pulling her into a kiss. The brazen approach wasn't what surprised her at first; it was how soft and full his lips were. She pushed into the kiss, enjoying the balance between the softness and the power behind them. She pushed him onto his back and straddled him, all without breaking the kiss.

"Oh God, that's hot," he moaned.

Her hips began to grind on him, and through her leggings and his jeans, she could feel how hard he was starting to become. She sat up straight and pulled her shirt off, and his hands trailed from her thighs, over her hips, up her stomach, to her breasts. His touch left a tingling trail that faded faster than she would have liked. He pulled her bra up over her breasts and started to circle her nipples with his thumbs. She lightly moaned in response, but all she could think about at that moment was how much the bra was uncomfortably pushing down on her tits. With one hand, she clipped one, two, three hooks, and threw her bra to the end of the bed. He pulled her chest down to him and replaced his thumbs with this tongue.

"That feels really good," she moaned sincerely.

"There's more where that came from," he said.

She replied with a slow grind of her hips, and he had to lay his head back on the pillow to moan. "Take off your pants," he instructed.

She rolled over and pulled her leggings off, pretending they weren't hard to get over her ankles. By the time she had removed them, Peter had taken his shirt and jeans off. He crawled back on top of her and went back to sucking on her sensitive nipples, while one of his hands trailed down to the heat of her that ached a little more with each passing second.

With just a little bit of teasing that made her quiver, he finally gave her exactly what she needed with just one finger. She gasped at how easily he'd found her most sensitive point and repaid him with breathy moans and a few slow and lazy circles before he slid down and into the hottest part of her.

"Oh God, you're so wet already," he groaned. He shoved his finger in and out once, twice, and used that same dripping-wet finger to circle around her favorite spot once more. The sensual heat of his breath on her neck and his meticulously slow pumping with his fingers in and out made her breath catch. Her vision started to blur as she tried to focus on a spot on the ceiling, as if using it as an anchor in this plane of existence as she seemed to drift away.

She came to when she felt his other hand take her wrist and draw it down toward the bulge growing in his underwear. She started a slow, rhythmic rubbing of his hard excitement, making the most of the friction created by the thin layer of cloth. He thrust into her hand and rocked his hips side to side, as if trying to get her to reach in through the slot of his boxers.

She tickled the skin where the waistband of his boxers pinched it, and once he gave her an agonizing growl of anticipation, she plunged her hand into his boxers, grabbing hold of his deliciously hard, warm, and, might she say, very large cock.

His breath caught in his throat, and she stopped him from rubbing her clit so that he could focus on thrusting into her hand. She shifted ever so slightly to reach deeper, so her fingers could reach the very base of his manhood.

He immediately froze. "Oh God. Oh no," he gasped. He quickly pulled away from her, rolled off the bed, and waddled out of the room. She heard a door close down the hallway and a distant groan.

She lay there in astonished bewilderment, trying to think of what she had just done to have caused him to run off. Did she accidentally scratch him with her nail; did she grip him too tightly; was her hand too dry?

She thought of all the minute details that had just transpired between them within the last five minutes to figure it out, but before she could, she was shocked out of her reverie when she heard a door open.

She rolled toward the door and propped herself up onto her elbow as she heard his feet approach the room.

"Sorry about that," he said.

"Are you all right; did I do something to you?"

"No, no. Not at all. I think I just suddenly got really tired and had to step away. I gotta work pretty early in the morning," he said.

She waited for him to say anything additional, but he just looked guiltily between her and the floor. "Yeah, you're right. I gotta work in the morning too."

"I can walk you out."

* * *

"He didn't let me cum!" Stacey yelled when she got back to Mary's apartment. The only light on was in the bedroom, and Stacey knew Mary was still up reading or scrolling through Instagram reels because she claimed to be too good for TikTok itself.

"What? Come in here. I'm too lazy to do a couch confessional right now."

Stacey clomped her way into Mary's room, flopped onto the foot of Mary's bed, planking-challenge style, and growled into the comforter. "The whole exchange was so hot, and I was so fucking close. And that's not the worst part!" She turned her head to look at Mary. She couldn't decipher what her blank expression meant, so she looked away and waited for Mary to ask for more.

"Go on. I'm listening."

"I was giving him…a hand," Stacey started and turned her head back toward Mary to watch in pleasant satisfaction as Mary rolled her eyes at the innuendo, "and he just jumped out of the bed and ran to the bathroom. I'm pretty sure I pushed a sweet spot pretty early on, and he had to relieve himself elsewhere out of embarrassment."

"You know, if you were actually doing the thing, the innuendo doesn't hold as much power."

"I was kind of hoping you were gonna be with me and say he was a literal two-pump chump, but all right."

"That part is obvious. So I'm guessing he didn't try to make up for it?"

"No! He kicked me out right after. He was, like, 'I have to work early tomorrow,'" she said in a mocking tone. "*Scott Pilgrim* lied to me, or else he would have turned into a pile of coins." She sighed and tucked her face into the comforter.

Mary huffed out a nose exhale and shook her head. "I mean, you weren't anticipating sleeping over, were you? I could tell it was going to be a 'wham, bam, thank you, ma'am' kind of situation, considering there wasn't much preamble leading up to you going over."

"No, but some cuddling would have been nice. It's starting to feel like doing this is making me more sexually frustrated than not having sex for two years."

"I get that. How was the sex at least?"

"We never made it that far."

"Wait! How did—" Mary started.

"UNO Reverse the innuendo," Stacey said flatly.

Mary blinked at her a few times while she processed what Stacey was saying. "Oh, so he never even…"

"That's what I'm trying to say! It was all so fast."

"Yikes. Do you think you'd want to try it again and try to not get him too excited too early next time?"

"Yeah no, after that awkward re-dressing and walking out, I'm good with just adding him to the list and moving on."

CHAPTER
8

"Thank goodness it's payday, am I right?" Stacey said as Lisa, Greg, and she meandered their way downstairs in the elevator at lunch. Because of the strict lunch schedule they had to follow for work, Stacey and Greg had no choice but to be stuck in the elevator with Lisa for two extra minutes than they would have liked.

Lisa dramatically rolled her eyes and put her nose to her phone after pressing the button for the ground level.

Sensing her annoyance, Greg replied to keep up the conversation, "Tell me about it. I put my couch on my credit card, and it never fails to remind me that I still have another five months left. I'm trying to make it only four, but a new video game came out, and I feel like it wouldn't hurt to add to my collection."

He looked over at Stacey, his eyes hovering over her chest as the button to her blouse threatened to burst with every breath she took. As if sensing him looking at her, she snuck a glance up with a raised eyebrow.

A half smile inched onto his face, and he gave her a quick wink while Lisa continued to look at her phone. Stacey's heart fluttered not so subtly, and her lips parted in a small "oh" of surprise. Greg's eyes quickly focused on them, and Stacey's breathing picked up.

"What about you, Lisa? You seem kind of quiet," Stacey said. The air grew colder suddenly, and to stop the animosity and break the silence, Stacey made a response as if Lisa had asked her that question. "I gotta admit, it's nice this week because I don't have any bills due, so I might make this weekend a salon weekend. My ends are looking like those bird-repellent spikes you see on shop signs."

It took Greg a moment to imagine it, and then he chuckled softly once it hit him.

Lisa gave Stacey a judgmental once-over and finally let out a scoffing laugh, as if she didn't want to give Stacey the satisfaction of having elicited a wholehearted laugh.

When Lisa stepped through the elevator doors as soon as they opened, Stacey gave her back a quick double-fisted one-finger salute.

"I thought it was funny," Greg reassured her.

"It's nice to be appreciated."

Through the wall of windows at the entrance of their building, they watched Lisa turn to the right, so Greg and

Stacey naturally decided to make a left toward the deli around the corner.

"Hopefully they have their loaded baked potato soup today," Stacey wished aloud.

"I've never actually had loaded baked potato soup. I'm honestly not a fan of soup in general."

"Well, that just means there's more for me."

"You know, I've never met a woman who would reply like that. Usually, they argue that my opinion is quite possibly the worst in the world, and then they go off on me about how I'm wrong. I'm sorry; I have a mind of my own," Greg said with a hint of aggressive annoyance at the end of his sentence.

Stacey absentmindedly nodded along with him. "That's actually the reason I say it the way I do. I've grown tired of people trying to push their preferences on me like I have the wrong one, and I started to hate myself whenever I did that to others. It's just so middle school, and that's a time in my life I'm trying to repress the memory of."

"All of us had a rough go in middle school, so I'm right there with ya, sistah," Greg said with the snap of his fingers in a Z formation.

"Please don't do that; it makes you lose some of your appeal."

"Oh? And what kind of appeal do you usually see me having?" he said, standing closer to her while they waited in line at the deli, hovering over her with a warm force field that was still comfortable in the stifling-hot shop.

She looked up into his eyes and gave him a sly smile. "The appeal of a man that enjoys making a girl always itch for a little more."

He leaned down a little farther, and his eyes slowly dropped back down to her chest as he enjoyed the angle of his vantage point.

She made her breaths a little deeper than necessary and started to nibble on her bottom lip.

"Next! You're up, lady!" the shopkeeper yelled at Stacey.

She jumped, and her forehead almost collided with Greg's nose. She stumbled through her order as the shopkeeper gave them an exasperated, disgruntled look as they placed their orders.

Ten minutes later, they walked back toward their building, and sat in the small, tree-shaded courtyard in between their building and the next. He sat and crossed his legs in that wide-open lap way guys do; she sat facing him with one knee on the bench seat, the other over the front of the bench.

"I see you didn't get the soup today," Greg said.

"It suddenly became too hot to want it anymore. So this chef salad will have to do."

"You can't handle the heat?"

"Not if I can't get relief from it," she said. She felt as if she was on a high as her confidence propelled further on its roll and swelled every time he looked at her. She internally patted herself on the back for her quick repartee.

He stopped chewing as he processed her response and shook his head in astonishment. "Here I was, thinking you were so hard to read for the longest time," he said.

It was her turn to stop chewing while she stared at him. "Well, that was back when I was with someone and didn't know how to show my true side, but I guess I can now come off as sassy and jaded as the best of them."

"It was a really shitty and terrible thing that happened to you, and you definitely did not deserve it, but I wouldn't say you were jaded."

"Excuse you?"

"I mean, yeah, he fucked you over, but it was more him showing his true side, which had nothing to do with you. So don't think you're jaded; think more of it as being relieved from possibly being stuck with a huge mistake," Greg said.

Stacey had heard countless times that it wasn't her fault for what Tyler did to her, but she'd never heard anyone word it like that. Her shoulders lifted as if she truly was relieved of all the bullshit he put her through, and saw Greg as a little bit more than just a frat boy once again. She realized she enjoyed getting to know this side of him, and wanted to know a few more sides of him, physically and metaphorically.

Without a second thought, she asked, "What are you up to tonight?"

If he was surprised by her boldness, he didn't show any sign of it. He swallowed his bite and gave her a smile before he said, "Absolutely nothing."

* * *

She stumbled backwards into Greg's apartment when he finally got the door unlocked and open. She found his lips once more as soon as the door closed behind them, and her hands greedily grabbed at his shirt. Her brain, swimming with desire and the aftereffects of three hard ciders and a tequila shot, bounced around the same three thoughts: *It is so fun sneaking around, I never realized just how sexy I could feel with someone,* and *Is he only doing this because I'm vulnerable?* She could feel her eyebrows scrunch together, relax, and then raise with a devilish flicker as each thought passed through her brain.

Once she heard Greg bolt the door, she dropped to her knees in a moment of sensual dominance. She undid his pants, pulled down his boxers, and took his already-swollen cock in her hand. She maintained eye contact with him as her tongue licked the length of him and she took his tip into her mouth.

He braced himself against the door and tangled his fingers in her hair. "Oh fuck, save some of me for you," he moaned. He pushed her far enough away to pull her up, walked her backwards a couple of steps, spun her, and bent her over the back of his couch.

* * *

"Did you put new sheets on the bed today or something?" Stacey asked as she rolled onto her back after checking her phone.

A message from Eric 2 had popped up, and her hand shook almost imperceptibly as a mini war waged inside her, torn between a sense of betrayal for both the man lying next to her and the one she had never met. She stuffed the feeling deep into her chest after replying to Eric 2 and looked back at Greg. After a little adjusting, she had sprawled out over the sheets, draping the corner of the top sheet over her stomach, while Greg lay on his back with nothing on but a smile.

"I did, actually. I feel like that's a weird thing to say right after fucking someone though."

Stacey couldn't help but blush at his matter-of-fact tone. "I've heard some really bad things after sex, and I feel saying something in general is a lot better than having an awkward silence hanging in the air."

"I'm a little worried to hear what else you've heard after sex."

"The most recent one was 'Well, I gotta work in the morning. See you around.'"

"Ouch. Do I want to know how recent?"

"You're not my gyno, so no," Stacey said.

Greg seemed a little miffed at her retort, which caught her off guard.

"But the worst were actually from my ex. I know, at the time, he said them mostly as a joke, but he would say them on more than one occasion. He was a fan of those medieval shows like *Game of Thrones*, so every now and then he would say 'gratitude' or 'that'll do.' After the fourth or fifth time of each, it got really old."

"Jesus, your ex would do that? Why didn't you dump his ass sooner?"

"Blind love and all that crap. I know it's not the best reason, but it's the only one I have right now."

"You weren't settling, were you?" he asked.

At first, she heard blood rushing in her ears at the thought that he had the nerve to say she'd settled, but Greg's eyes were soft, and his lips were slightly parted as if he was about to say something else.

Before she could defend herself, he said, "You deserve so much better than someone you have to settle for. You should never settle; you're too good for that."

She stared at Greg with wide eyes and tried to see if there was a punch line coming at any point. She waited through three breaths and a confused eyebrow raise before she realized there wasn't a punch line coming.

"Did I say something wrong?" Greg said to break the quiet.

She replied with a deep and long kiss that she held as she straddled him.

CHAPTER
9

As soon as she made it home from work that Friday, she pulled a bottle of hard cider out of the fridge and had the cap tinkling on the counter before the door to the fridge closed. She trudged to the couch and flopped onto the cushion of her designated side. After she finished half the bottle, she kicked off her heels and started to massage the balls of her feet, which hurt but were numb, all at the same time.

As she sipped at her bottle, she tried to count all the reasons she loved her job and had stayed with the company for three years; Steve definitely wasn't one of the reasons, and Lisa didn't help things, especially when one was known for unprofessionally tearing you down, and the other would do anything to keep you from getting the promotion for which you'd been gunning.

The more Stacey thought about Lisa, the more absent-minded sips she took. She only noticed her bottle was empty when she swallowed air. Stacey released an exasperated groan as she stood up and popped open a second bottle. To get her mind off the twat of a coworker, she decided to swipe through Tinder for a little bit.

The very first profile she saw was obviously a fake account, complete with each picture either being photoshoot posed or on a green screen with poorly done Photoshop; the edge between the man and the background was blurred as if he was surrounded by the background, not in front of it.

She swiped left, only to find a fish picture. Stacey was frustratingly picking up on the fact that men apparently think women enjoy seeing them hold something too small to be proud of. Another swipe to the left, and Stacey found a profile of a man who seemed dorky yet hot, claimed he enjoyed reading, and golfing on weekends. There were pictures of a loving group who looked like his family and of him with friends at a petting zoo. Then one of the prompts made her pause; it mentioned something about "ENM," and she couldn't pick up the context clues from the rest of his answer to figure out what it meant.

A quick search on Google gave her the answer; she was not happy. "Gods, I should add 'are poly' to the list of why it's so hard to find a guy these days. So much for only having 'gay' or 'taken' on that list," Stacey muttered into her bottle.

Halfway through her Tinder search, Mary walked in. She took one look at Stacey's swollen feet next to the empty bottle on the coffee table, and at the raging fire in Stacey's eyes, and simply gave her a knowing nod. "Lisa?"

"Lisa," Stacey echoed into her bottle.

Mary wandered into the kitchen, and Stacey heard the *shnk* of the breaking seal on the fridge, the *crack... fizz* of a hard seltzer being opened, and the light *fwop-fwop* of Mary's ballet-flat footsteps as she made her way to the couch. "I think it's time to go out again. It's been—what?—three weeks?"

"We aren't in college anymore. I don't know how much more I can go out to the clubs."

"Listen here, old woman. We're going out, and you're going to like it. Besides, you're going to want to be moving with that buzz you're going to have soon," Mary said as she motioned between the empty bottle and the one in Stacey's hand.

Stacey simply gave her a noncommittal shrug and gulped down the rest of her bottle.

"Now, tell Mama who pushed you on the playground. I need to know who to throw shade at, at the next PTA meeting."

"I'll need another drink."

"Nope, not until you tell me. Don't need you drunk already for this story time."

Stacey brought her hands up to her lips in a praying motion, took a deep breath, and with just the flick of her wrist, karate-chopped the air to enhance the emphasis on the start of her story.

"So...Lisa was on some next-level undermining today, and of course she had to do it in front of Steve, and even in front of the printing-press representative that happened to come in today to talk about where they are headed with production and costs and everything. And then I mumbled under my breath something about the price of the magazine already being too high because they use fancy eco-friendly paper, and of course Lisa heard me and had to point out that I said something, and then went on to say that I also said that nobody cares about the eco-friendly paper they use, and that's why I felt continuing on with a printing press that doesn't take into consideration that being cost-conscious is just as important as eco-friendly wasn't ethical.

"They all looked at *me* like I had three heads, even though she's the one that said it. Then they turned the meeting around to how a winning mindset starts from within and this, that, and the other thing, and *then*, oh my God, *then*, when the meeting was over, Steve met with me to talk about my feelings and how it was inappropriate to bring them up in front of a client the way I did and that it was my second mark that he would have to put on my record for insubordination.

"But I honestly don't even remember the first one, and when I tried to argue that it was all Lisa's doing, he didn't want to hear anything in his misogynistic way, as if I had already made a fool of myself and should sit in the corner, look pretty, and think about what I did.

"It's all so fucked, Mary. I really can't stand that bitch anymore. I really wish I could claw her eyes out and push her out the window," Stacey rushed out in just two breaths. She huffed a couple of times to help her heart and lungs regain a normal balance between rhythm and air.

Mary snapped her jaw shut, blinked her eyes a couple of times in astonishment, and sighed. "Well, I think it's time for that other drink." She got up quickly and practically ran to the fridge.

Stacey looked down at her empty bottle and felt lightheaded, but relieved at the same time. She had told Mary plenty of times in the past about the way Lisa's hooves clomp around her, but it was an overdue relief to have a solid example to give Mary in order to fully express and prove just how terrible a person Lisa was. Sure, her shoulders still shook in shame every time she thought about Steve's face when he talked *at* her, but her appreciation for Mary overshadowed anything she had gone through that day, that month, and in the last six years that they had known one another.

Stacey was so deep in thought that she jumped when Mary shoved a glass of something bright blue in her face. She blinked a couple of times before she took the already-sweating glass and sniffed its contents. Sophomore year of college came rushing back to her in a bittersweet, but mostly nauseating, wave. She took a tentative sip and was assaulted with the burning power of cheap vodka; that was soon overpowered by the overly sweet blend of blue raspberry and carbonated citrus. A shiver ran down her spine in disgust at how much she was enjoying it.

"When did you get this vodka? I thought they only sold it to girls with fake IDs since that's the only people they seem to market to."

"I was feeling nostalgic the other day when I went to the liquor store." Mary tipped back her own glass slowly.

Stacey had to hold back a laugh when she saw Mary gag ever so slightly when she finished it.

"Gods, this reminds me of that one time this guy danced on me at a house party, and wouldn't get the hint that I wasn't a fan of his anatomy and proximity," Mary said. She took another jarring sip and let her shoulders drop.

Stacey took a gulp and hunkered down on the couch. "For me? It reminds me of pregaming awkwardly with my roommate in her fling's dorm room before going out and partying, and how she would leave me so she could fuck him somewhere in the house we ended up in."

"There's no way they fucked in every house," Mary said incredulously.

"I mean, heavily making out on a couch next to you is the same thing, right?"

"You know you could have hung out with me instead."

Stacey gave her a noncommittal shoulder shrug before replying, "It was before I met you. I think they officially broke up because he was bored with her, like, a week before we met," Stacey said.

Mary's eyes flickered, and her mouth moved without producing any sound. Stacey could envision math problems hovering around Mary's head; they changed every time her eyes moved.

"So they were together for, like, three months." More mental math. "That's like two years in college time."

"Honestly, I'm surprised they lasted that long because they were two completely different people; she was there to have a good time while busting her back trying to make her grades, and he was just there to bust on girls' backs." Stacey tipped her head back for another sip, but was greeted with ice to the teeth and nose. She gave the glass a little shake.

Mary dramatically rolled her eyes; her head rolled with the force. "Another one coming right up, milady. Then we are getting our happy asses ready for a night out. I think you could use it."

* * *

Two hours later, they each took a final look in the large mirror over Mary's dresser. Before them was a glittery graveyard that would have put any preteen in her Wet 'n Wild days to shame. Stacey brushed a little more bronzer on her chest to give more shape to her breasts and grew frustrated when the results weren't as bold as she wanted.

"The reason it's not working is because you already have enough goods to work with; any more will make you look like the silicone is trying to break out of the skin," Mary said without looking at her, as if sensing Stacey's frustration.

Stacey threw the brush at her and moved her attention to her hair. "We should get going if we want to actually get into the bar before a line forms out the door," she said as she used some hair spray.

Hey beautiful. How was your day? Eric 2 messaged Stacey.

She felt tingly with schoolgirl giddiness when she saw his name pop up on the screen; they had talked a bit more seriously the last few days, more than they had over the last two weeks they had been talking. She couldn't get over how gentlemanly he was. She tamped down the concern that they still hadn't made any plans to actually meet; she tried not to let it get to her too much.

With another sip of her blue-raspberry cocktail, she typed: *Hey handsome. It was a long day to say the least, but thankfully it's Friday so I have a chance to recharge over the weekend*

I hear you there. I get to see my daughter tonight and she always makes my day instantly better the moment I see her smile

Awww, that's so cute. In your defense, she is really adorable

They gushed back and forth, and just when Stacey was starting to have an actual conversation with him, Mary pulled on her elbow and led her toward the door.

"You and lover boy can wait five minutes. We gotta go before this buzz wears off."

* * *

Eric 2: *The beach is always a first choice for me. I love the sun, the heat. It would be perfect if you were sunbathing next to me on the beach ;)*

Stacey touched her cheeks, thinking it would hide the vibrant blush that crept over her face. She felt good, she had to admit, in a lot of ways: the alcohol hitting her in a fuzzy-headed, fingertip-tingly stupor; talking with an actual man who was saying all the right things without being prompted; and partying with her best friend in the world for whom she would take a bullet.

She looked over at Mary, who was nodding her head like and swinging her hips, and watched as she tipped her head back to confidently sing along with the rest of the bar as the chorus bumped out of the speakers. Although her head was swimming, she followed along with the wave of arms as the song continued.

Once the song was over, she checked her phone and noticed that there wasn't a new message from Eric 2. Her eyebrows furrowed, and she shakily opened her messages to see that he'd read her message five minutes before. "But he's been messaging back within seconds," she slurred under her breath.

Mary turned her attention from singing about her best friend's mom and tried to piece together what Stacey was saying and make out her friend's expression. "What's wrong?" she asked as her sloshed brain recognized sadness.

"He left me on read!"

"Maybe he's tucking his daughter in. You said he had her tonight, didn't you?"

"Yeah, but I feel like he would have told me." Stacey sucked on the vodka-flavored ice water at the bottom of her glass and swayed as she leaned on the bar.

Drunk me noticed you left me on read, Stacey finally managed after a couple of attempts.

Within seconds, she saw the ellipsis pop up, and after what felt like an hour, he replied, *Haha, well I figured you wouldn't want me bothering you while you were out with your friends*

She was all at once both hurt and enamored as she read the message. "He didn't want to bother me while we're out! That's so sweet! But he's too hot to not text back to. I have to tell him that! It's so clever!"

She anxiously waited for his reply, and when he finally did, it was simply: *Lol glad you're having fun*, which was the last thing she remembered from the night.

* * *

"I'm too old for this shit," Mary said from her side of the bed. She was underneath one of her pillows in a suffocating attempt to block out the sun streaming through her blinds.

"Get curtains. I keep telling you this. You're not too old for common sense, are you?" Stacey strained to get out, scratchy throat notwithstanding. She made a smacking sound with her tongue to assess just how badly she needed water and was heartbroken to realize that she'd have to leave the bed in order to stay alive.

With a groan, she rolled over and out of the bed, still in the clothes she'd worn to go out the night before. With a fumbling adjustment of the jeans and blouse so they were both facing forward, she clomped out of the bedroom and into the kitchen. Her stomach roiled threateningly, and she had a hard time keeping her eyes open.

After drinking some water, she returned to her bedroom and flopped back onto the bed, ignoring the creak and pain-filled groan. She picked her phone up from the nightstand and scrolled through her messages after she saw that she didn't have any new ones waiting for her. She opened the last one—she didn't remember sending it to Eric 2—and echoed Mary with the same painful groan.

I'm lamme i justt ordered watger stared back at her in bold and black Helvetica.

"What the fuck is wrong with me?" Stacey said, almost screaming. The effort and condition of her throat resulted in the croak of a 150-year-old witch who had just awakened from her hibernation.

Mary sat up straight in bed, eyes wide, and studied Stacey's face with a look of concern and confusion flashing over her own. "What the fuck was that? You sounded like the aunts from *The Simpsons*," she said.

Content with the resulting middle finger she received, Mary flopped back onto her side, facing Stacey. "What happened?" Mary asked again when Stacey did nothing but rub her face with her hands.

"I'm fucking done with myself. Read and then shoot me in the alley out back."

Mary grabbed the phone awkwardly, and it not so gracefully fell on her face before she dramatically squinted at the screen. "I don't think there is enough air in the world to voice the number of *o*'s I'd use in the word 'yo,'" Mary said.

Stacey shoved her face into the pillow beneath her hands and released a groan. "This is why I don't have that big of a track record. I'm too bloody weird."

"Hopefully he'll laugh it off the same way you'll laugh it off," Mary said. But after a glare from Stacey that pierced her soul, she hastily added, "In a couple of years."

Stacey punched Mary's arm, and they both began to laugh.

"See, you're laughing it off already. Now, I'm going to get into the shower first because it's my place, and then we'll do some retail therapy."

CHAPTER
10

Rank these three shows: Always Sunny in Philadelphia, Arrested Development, Bojack Horseman

Stacey had to blink through her surprised confusion as she scrolled back up to see what the man's profile said he was interested in.

It did say "Interested in Women." I'm not imagining it, she thought to herself.

Before she could ponder how much it felt that he was trying to actually attract dude bros, she swiped left. Only to immediately come face-to-face with the third close-up of just a man's abs. She admired them for a moment or three, shamelessly lingering on another picture that was of him flexing in a gym mirror, and then swiped right for the fun of it. Nothing popped up but the next profile, so she simply shrugged and continued on.

"You'll know I like you if: I let you meet my dog," one of the prompts said on the current profile. One of the corners of her mouth curled up as she enjoyed how light-hearted and cute that prompt answer was. She dragged her thumb to see more, and immediately after that prompt was a white, curly-haired, red, crusty-eyed dog sitting in the man's lap.

Left.

The very first picture of the next prompt was dark and blurry, with a random smiley face emoji over part of his face, but Stacey could still make out that the man had a joint in his mouth underneath his attempt at a censor bar and a raised middle finger with kitchen-job tattoos.

Left.

The next profile was just of random sunsets and a couple of prompts he had keyboard pounded just to put something in them.

Left.

The next one was lighthearted and well-balanced, with one picture of him hanging with friends, one of his family during a holiday, one of him walking his dog, and the obligatory swim-trunk picture at the end.

"I'll fall for you if you: play with my hair," read one of the prompts.

She swiped right, and it immediately popped up that they were a match.

Be witty; you can do it, she encouraged herself.

I'm taking a poll: what are your thoughts on pineapple on pizza? she typed. As much as she hated to admit it, she really enjoyed that icebreaker and had used it on a couple of other matches, with varying levels of reciprocation.

The train started to slow, and she stood up to prepare to run off.

* * *

As soon as she made it to her cubicle at work ten minutes later, she realized there was an odd level of chatter that wasn't normal for a Monday morning. She heard someone a row over say they hated how they had to "do this" every year.

She logged into her computer and immediately realized what the fuss was about: sexual-harassment training. "With a Twist!" the subject line stated. The email from the HR rep Jason said:

Good morning, everyone! It is that time of year again to refresh yourselves on our company's policy on sexual harassment and discrimination. We know it's a very heavy topic, but to help everyone remember it better, we will be conducting the training a little bit differently this year: audience participation! I have sent you your own line to respond with, according to the topic. When it gets to your turn, put those Juilliard graduates *to shame!*She wasn't sure which she hated more, the email itself or the line she was in charge of saying.

* * *

"Hey-ey, Stacey, you old dog! You get any this weekend?" Jason the HR rep loudly said to her as he passed her desk. He looked around to the other cubicles to see if others had started to pop their heads up. With an eye twitch to the two people who had looked, he gave Stacey a quick nod of encouragement.

"Jason, I don't appreciate you asking me that. It is inappropriate for work," Stacey replied in a theatrically loud and canned tone.

"See, everyone, that was the perfect response to my advance. Now, if this was a repeat offense, what should Stacey do next?" he asked the uninterested office.

He pointed to a random person on the other side of the room, who yelled out, "She needs to go to you to report it."

"That's exactly right. From there, I will take the next necessary step, which may result in a write-up of the harasser, or even termination."

"Are you going to write yourself up? You seem to do a lot of these things yourself already. I don't know if writing yourself up will stop you," Lisa yelled from her chair.

Jason grew bright red and took a couple of breaths before he responded, "That is another perfect example of what not to say in the office. Thank you for offering that, Lisa."

"Oh, I wasn't offering; that's sincere."

The scattered, restrained chuckles grew to actual laughs, and Jason's head turned into a red balloon, bobbing awkwardly as he looked around to see the stifled grins on almost everyone's face.

"Do we have a conference meeting coming up for you to explain more examples right now?" Stacey said to break the tension.

Jason just gave her a couple of terse nods, and with one final warning glare at Lisa, he turned toward another row of cubicles for the next scripted scenario.

"You know he enjoys his handwriting just as much as he enjoys hearing himself talk, right?" Greg said to Lisa over their divider.

"I think he's just upset that I embarrassed him in front of everyone," Lisa said.

"I don't know which question to ask first: how do you know he's upset about being embarrassed, or why do you care?" Greg said, dramatically counting on his fingers with each one.

"I mean, we're hooking up, so that could be the reason why I care," Lisa said without a moment's hesitation.

Stacey and Greg stared gape-mouthed for a few uncomfortable moments before Lisa laughed.

"What? We signed the paperwork and everything, so messing with him like that doesn't count, right?" she said. Fear suddenly flashed in her eyes, and her smile fell. "Right?" she asked again as if to convince herself. The deflation in her face and shoulders made Stacey's heart swell and almost beat out of her chest with satisfaction that Lisa could in fact feel embarrassment.

Stacey simply gave Lisa a noncommittal shrug and stood up to dramatically look down at her. "Lisa, I don't appreciate you asking me that. It is inappropriate for work," Stacey said in the same canned tone she had used the first time.

Lisa quickly stood and practically sprinted away as if she could hide how her blush had covered her whole face.

Stacey doubled over and quietly laughed to herself. When she righted herself, she wiped away a tear that had lingered in her eyelash.

Greg made his way over to her and tilted his head to the side in stunned confusion. "God, that was so fucking beautiful. I didn't think she had any emotions besides raging bitch," Greg said.

"Honestly, it would explain why she does end up getting away with a lot of the shit she has said and done. Jason must just sweep it under the rug, and Lisa acts like it never happened."

"I feel more unsafe now than before, unfortunately."

"Bring it up to your HR rep. Oh wait..." Stacey said as another wave of celebratory yet baffled giggles bubbled to her throat.

"So I guess that means we can't be asking others if they got any over the weekend. Which is unfortunate because that's what I was going to ask you," Greg said in a softer tone.

The heat of his body next to hers and his breathy tone of voice shot a shiver up her back. "I don't appreciate you asking me that; that is inappropriate for work," she said in a matching tone. "But definitely a topic that can be discussed outside of work," she added. She gave him a slow grin over her shoulder before she walked ahead of him, and she had to admit that surprised little parting of his lips made something start to roil inside her—more specifically, in her skirt.

"If you really must know, I did get some over the weekend," Stacey said later that night. She was wearing Greg's sheet, and he was just wearing the leg she had spooned over his own.

He wiped from his forehead a little more sweat than he would have admitted to and used the same hand to urge Stacey to give more information.

"Saturday night. I had to go to his place because I'm still living with my friend, and I will admit I wasn't all for it at first because I was still pretty hungover from the night before."

"And you're already in my bed again? Alpha status, ba-by!" He whooped with a flex of the arm opposite Stacey.

She lightly slapped his chest and rolled her eyes.

A little miffed, he cleared his throat and continued, "Was it even worth it in that case? For guys, I have to say, it's almost always worth it because it's sex, but I know women are a lot more sensitive about that kind of thing," Greg said.

Stacey propped herself onto her elbow and glared down at him. "What do you mean, more sensitive? We like sex too. Contrary to popular belief, we think about it just as much as guys do. If not more, but our bodies don't give us away when we do."

He held up two hands in surrender and chuckled softly. "I'm just saying a lot of girls I've been with have always needed to be like one hundred percent in the mood. How bad did you fake it?"

"You should know," Stacey said teasingly.

Greg mimed stabbing himself in the heart, and they both fell into a fit of giggles. Stacey's breath caught for the smallest moment when she realized just how much she enjoyed how natural and simple it was to be doing this with Greg. She flopped back onto the bed in a casual attempt to hide the blush invading her face.

"I guess, in a way it was."

"What do you mean, 'you guess'?" Greg asked.

Stacey took a deep breath and counted to three in order to buy time to think of a lie to replace the fact that her Saturday night hookup was the letter *H*.

"He went down on me for pretty much the whole time. But, honestly, I'm not the biggest fan," Stacey said.

Greg beamed a little, and a sly grin creased the right side of his face. "Not that big a fan, huh? Guess I'm going to have to prove that wrong."

"Do what you will, but grinding on a dick is better than a tongue any day."

"I sense a challenge that I am prepared to take up!" Greg exclaimed as he rolled over on top of her and started nuzzling her neck.

Stacey had to admit to herself that she was all too sensitive to the feeling of his hand slowly pulling off the sheet and teasingly making its way down her body.

* * *

Stacey dropped her keys to Mary's apartment on the side table just inside the front door and made a beeline to the fridge. She gave a quick wave to a green-clay-masked Mary sitting cross-legged on the couch with a laptop on her legs.

"You want one?"

"I don't know what it is, but I trust you."

Stacey walked back around the couch and handed Mary the second hard cider she'd grabbed from the kitchen.

"How was your day?" Stacey asked as she dramatically thunked both feet individually onto the coffee table.

Mary looked between Stacey and her feet on the table very Old Spice commercial-like and shook her head in defeat. "It wasn't too bad. I had the chance to work with some clients one-on-one today, but it also made me realize that I refer to the fancy names of colors over the actual colors. Like cerulean instead of light blue."

"But those are two completely different things."

"Fucking tell me about it. But that's why I'm working for the client, because they haven't the foggiest of what they want." Mary took a sip of her bottle and analyzed Stacey's ruffled hair, the missing statement necklace that had matched her skirt perfectly when she saw it on her that morning, and her dopey look.

"And how was your day?" she asked as if she already knew.

"We had sexual-harassment training today. I had a hot dog from that one cart today and instantly regretted it, found out Lisa's fucking Jason, and I hooked up with Greg again."

Mary did a spit take into her hand, to avoid getting anything on her laptop, and gasped for air. "Wait, hol' up. Lisa is hooking up with Jason? The HR rep? I feel like that is wrong on so many levels, mostly the level that she is actually getting any and is still a raging twat."

"Out of all of that, the main takeaway was Lisa? Not the fact I got a hot dog? The nerve of some people." Stacey jokingly crossed her arms over her chest and huffed.

"Bitch, I will kick you off this couch if you don't spill right now."

"Damn, who got your panties in a twist?" Stacey asked.

The look Mary gave her in response froze her soul and curdled her blood all at once.

"All right, all right. We were doing the harassment training, and she said something really inappropriate to Jason, and he just walked away. She was unfazed about the consequences, and she was only upset she 'embarrassed him like that,' and she was fine because they were hooking up, with signatures and everything. She was so nonchalant about it at first, but you should have seen her face when she realized she'd told us."

"Us?"

"Greg and me."

"Speaking of which, I kind of figured you were with him tonight. I was half tempted to make it look like I had been waiting for you to come home, but then work reminded me that I am now salary."

"Thanks, Mom, but I'm a big girl; let me do my walk of shame on my own," Stacey said before finishing her bottle.

She took in a deep breath and watched a waterdrop race down the side as she tried to piece together how to tell Mary how she was feeling. She loved Mary dearly, but knew that she wouldn't be too kind to hear that she may or may not be falling for her frat-boy coworker. As she watched another waterdrop roll its way down the glass, she sensed Mary grow quiet beside her.

"Oh God, you like him, don't you?" Mary asked quietly as if she could read Stacey's mind.

Her heart started to pound, but she wasn't sure if she liked the sensation because she worried about what Mary would have to say next about it. Stacey couldn't meet Mary's eyes, so she simply gave a small nod.

Mary grew silent once again, drew in a deep breath, and buzzed her lips as she let her breath out. "I don't know what to say, kid. Is it because you've been hooking up, or because he's an actual functioning civilian?" Mary asked.

Stacey released a cross between a scoff and a laugh of relief that Mary hadn't completely jumped down her throat. "A little of both maybe? Have I told you that his place has always been clean whenever I go over? Either he was the grunt boy of the house, or he is actually a fully functioning adult. Hell, I'm pretty sure if I was living on my own, I wouldn't be as clean as he is."

"I mean, even living with someone, you aren't the cleanest," Mary said with a smirk.

Stacey pretended to throw her empty bottle at her, and they both fell into a fit of giggles.

CHAPTER

11

I really want to see you ;) I want to see those beautiful eyes in person. Are you available tonight?

I am ;) maybe we can meet up at a bar or something near you?

I don't really have anything around me. Maybe we can just hang out at my place?

We can do that too. We can probably watch a movie on Netflix or something. I'll bring the popcorn!

That sounds good. But you can have the popcorn. I'll be busy eating something else that starts with the letter p ;)

Stacey stared down at her phone for a solid minute, holding back the bile that had risen up her throat. A new Tinder match she received that following Friday night, by the name of Will, had messaged her first. After a total of maybe thirty interactions between the two of them, he was already messaging a suggestion that she would be screaming his name. And now he would be "eating something else that starts with the letter *P*"?

She swallowed down both the bile and her dignity when she simply replied that she couldn't wait with a winking face. He was the first guy with a name that started with the letter *W*, and she didn't want to let the opportunity pass. She did have to admit that he was pretty cute in most of his pictures, and the one with the well-maintained beard and muscular shoulders had won her over.

When he simply replied with yet another winking face, she locked her phone and pushed it to the other side of her desk.

"Another Tinder match ignore you? Guys just don't like it when you message them first, you know," Lisa said as she wandered back from the break room with a cup of coffee.

"They also think that putting a winking face anywhere in a message is an invitation to fuck, so there's no happy in-between, I guess," Stacey shot back.

Greg cleared his throat at his desk, and his keyboard grew quiet for the smallest of moments.

"I'm surprised because everyone can see that you're a prude from a mile away," Lisa responded.

"Which is funny considering the number of guys I've hooked up with since the breakup, your dad included," Stacey said nonchalantly.

Greg's head whipped toward her so quickly she was sure she heard his neck crack, and she sensed a few of the people in the cubicle cluster across the way had poked their heads up to get a better view of the show.

Lisa's face twisted and took on a terrifying shade of... not red, but...blue, as if she had had an aneurysm. Something flickered in her eyes, and her face shifted from anger to condescension.

"Human names you've given to dildos don't count," Lisa said matter-of-factly, not even taking her eyes off her computer screen.

Stacey mentally applauded Lisa, but she immediately turned on herself for even thinking that Lisa deserved any sort of accolade for being a bitch.

A round of "oohhs" hummed from the cluster, amping up the hype for the crowd currently watching the roast battle taking place in their office.

"At least they can get me off so I'm not a raging twat to my coworkers because I have to always fake it to keep my job," Stacey shot back. She kicked herself for how much she was grasping at that, but swelled with pride when she saw Lisa's shoulders stiffen and hunch over her coffee.

Greg popped his head over his divider, and his amused face quickly grew worried when he saw Lisa's face. He shot a warning glance to Stacey, and her blood started to run cold.

Lisa slowly turned around in her chair and practically punched Stacey in the face with force of her glare. Lisa's face didn't move for what felt like five minutes; then she stood up and slowly walked toward the elevator.

"Jesus, if looks could kill," Stacey said. Part of her shivered in fear of not knowing what Lisa was going to do.

"I think I saw actual flames flicker in her eyes when I looked. But I have to admit that was a pretty good one," Greg said. He lifted his fist up.

Stacey gave him a limp air fist bump, and she spun back to her computer, worry blurring her vision as she tried to concentrate on her emails. As she was reading through her article on price matching throw pillows between two department stores, her work phone rang. Jason's name blazed on caller ID, and she took a few calming breaths before she answered.

"Hey, Stacey, how are ya?" Jason asked.

"I'm good, just working on an article. You know, occupational hazard." Stacey chuckled. She heard dead air from the other end, so she loudly cleared her throat and asked him the same.

"I'm good; I'm good. Not too bad, can't complain. Really enjoying the weather out there today. But, hey, there's work that needs to be done. Is there any chance you can come up for a moment? It won't take long; you'll be back to your article in no time."

* * *

"So wait, you didn't get fired?" Mary asked. Stacey heard her muttering, "Excuse me," over the blaring horns and chatter in the background on her end of the phone.

Stacey gave another wail in reply from her pillow on the couch; she already felt defeated and hurt, but having her best friend just dismiss the fact that she was going to be closely monitored for the next two weeks to decide if she should be fired or not hurt her a little bit more.

"It's the principle; I can never seem to get ahead at that place, and that twat just makes things so much harder to even think about trying to make it work. The anxiety and fear of being expendable isn't nice, Mary."

"I'm not saying that it is. But you weren't completely fired, which is definitely a plus," Mary said.

Stacey rolled onto her back on the couch and sighed. "I guess I'm overreacting. Thanks for helping me see that," Stacey said sarcastically before tapping the End button on her phone. She let it fall onto her chest, and a small whimper slipped out. "Must be nice to have a nice, cushy, and safe job that was guaranteed to you with only half the amount of schooling. Real cool!" Stacey yelled into the empty apartment.

She heard a tapping followed by a muffled voice yelling from the ceiling and realized her neighbor had just heard her. "You can fuck off too!" she shouted, which resulted in another round of taps.

She rotated back onto her stomach and released a sigh with the force a trumpet player would be proud of. Her phone buzzed and chimed with an app alert, but she simply stared at the floor and followed paths in the grains of the hardwood. The lines began to blur as a wave of frustrated tears started to fill her eyes, but their surface tension never let them roll down her cheeks.

Her phone chimed an app tone again, and she was half tempted to chuck it across the room. Instead, she limply raised her arm, grabbed her phone, and blinked a few times to bring the notification into focus.

Will: *When do you think you'll be by tonight? ;)*

That time, she really was tempted to chuck the phone across the room.

I have to stay late for work tonight but we'll definitely have to choose a new time real soon.

After struggling to type and send the message, she flicked off the ringer switch and released a breath of relief when it simply vibrated back at her a moment later.

* * *

As Stacey walked out of the bathroom after washing her face, Mary was walking in with a bulging paper bag in her arms and an annoyed look on her face. "How dare you hang up on me, you cootie queen."

"Yeah well, I figured you weren't really listening because of how loud it was on your end, and you probably don't understand."

"You hanging up on me isn't going to help me understand. I'm sorry you got almost-fired today? What else was I supposed to say?"

"That Lisa is a fucking jerk and that you support me, and say a couple of nice words to smooth it out a little, instead of making a joke of it! I'm sorry I show my emotions a bit differently than you do, but receiving some support just because you're my friend would have been nice."

"And I didn't have a chance to know that because you hung up on me! See how that works? Look, I'm sorry today was a shitty day, and I really hope things smooth out soon. How about that?"

"It doesn't sound as sincere, but sure, thank you."

"If you see what is in the bag, you will feel like it's a little more sincere," Mary said.

Stacey looked from Mary to the bag and back to her again and waved her hand as if to say, "Well, show me."

Mary pulled out a bottle of peach liqueur, lemon- and raspberry-flavored vodkas, and a bottle of tea. She raised an eyebrow in anticipation of Stacey's response.

"You DO care for me! Why didn't you tell me that's what was in the bag?" Stacey looked at Mary, who nodded her head in exasperation. "Yeah, yeah, it's because I hung up on you." She made a beeline for the bottle of peach liqueur and started drinking it as soon as it was cracked open.

"Please tell me you will be adding that to something. That has, like, no alcohol content, my dude."

"Do we still have any hard iced teas left?" Stacey asked between gulps.

Mary wandered over to the small pantry and pulled out a six-pack of bottles. "They may not be cold, but that's what ice is for." As she said it, Mary had one cracked open and poured in a glass. She plucked the peach liqueur out of Stacey's grip and topped it off before struggling to add a couple of fresh-from-the-tray ice cubes. As if leading a horse with a carrot on a string, she made Stacey follow her to the couch before she finally gave her the drink.

"So tell your therapist what happened at school today," Mary said as she joined Stacey on the sofa.

"So she told her boyfriend on me, and I was called up to his office, shitting myself the whole time."

"Because you said a few mean things that weren't nearly as mean as what she said?"

"When you put it that way, it sounds juvenile, but yes."

"So she can dish it out, but she can't take it? I hope she pretends to choke on his tiny dick later, and then actually chokes on her shitty personality. So what exactly was said, though, because it still sounds really fucking catty."

Stacey took in a deep breath and then went over every detail, including the Lisa's dildo line and how Greg seemed a little worried about Lisa. She watched as Mary's face grew more and more puckered as she spoke. With another cleansing breath, and after a quick hiccup, Stacey went back to her drink.

"Jesus, me, and Joseph. That truly is a new low for her. Does she feel threatened by you?"

Stacey replied with a shrug.

"What about that position that was opening up because that one chick decided not to come back after her maternity leave?"

Stacey replied with another shrug. "I guess it's a sign that this isn't supposed to be the year I get anywhere in life. First Tyler, now my job. What's next? One of my parents will die?"

"I wouldn't see it as life trying to beat you down, as much as it is trying to tell you that you can do better. That magazine is dying out anyway, Tyler was and always will be a tool, and you deserve a lot better. Hell, think of it as a chance to finally start getting back to reading your to-be-read pile on your metaphorical shelf."

Stacey groaned and flopped her head onto the back of the couch. She tried to think of anything that she could do in place of working for the magazine, which had given her more experience than she ever thought she would get. Nothing but living on the sidewalk came to mind. Her breath grew shorter and faster as a panic attack overcame her without notice.

"Give. Me. More. Alcohol!" she cried.

Startled by the *Exorcist* tone in Stacey's voice, Mary jumped up and ran to the kitchen to throw together another drink.

CHAPTER
12

"It's nice to finally get the chance to see you," Will said as he opened the door.

Stacey was a little keyed up after having to take a train to Long Island to get to Will, which entailed getting lost and getting off two exits after where she needed to be.

"You too! This is such a nice house you have."

She kicked off one of her shoes and looked up to see two middle-aged faces staring at her from the living room. She stopped short while kicking the second shoe off and gaped at Will in search of some sort of answer as to what was going on.

"It's actually my parents' house. That's them in the living room."

"What the ACTUAL fuck is going on?" she hoped her eyes said to him.

He gave a weak shrug of his shoulders.

His father started to stand up, but Will just waved at them and led Stacey upstairs to his bedroom. He closed the door behind them, and she looked around, pleasantly surprised by how bare his room was; there was just one poster of a car, some baseball Pop Vinyl figures, and one tall and thin bookshelf that held every movie a dude was supposed to own if he wanted to keep his man card, like *Fight Club*, *Boondock Saints*, and *Friday the 13th*. He sat at the head of his twin-size bed, off to one of the sides as if to leave room for her, and he turned off his TV. She mentally calculated whether the bed or the computer chair was the better seat, and finally decided on the bed next to him.

"So you live with your parents. That's a nice money saver because apartments aren't cheap," Stacey said, trying to break the ice.

"Yeah, it's not too bad, even though I will admit it would be nice to just relax and not be told to do dishes." He laughed.

She chuckled with him, but each chuckle caused her skin to crawl.

"So where do you live?" he asked.

"I live in the city with a friend of mine. The apartment is small, but it's home for now."

"That's pretty cool! So you work in the city then?"

"Yeah, it's pretty nice actually. I live about a ten-minute train ride from my job. I have to walk a block to get to the subway both ways, but it's nice."

"Where do you work?"

"I edit and write for an interior design magazine that specializes in DIY and frugal alternatives. What about you? Do you work close to here?"

"Not too close, but I work with my dad at the school the next town over, as a custodian. Since I don't have a car, it kinda works out, so we drive to work together."

"That's pretty smart. So what movies do you like to watch?" she asked. She tried to keep each breath even to mask the fact that she was actually about to have a judgmental panic attack.

She thought she'd blacked out a little after he said he worked with his father, but it was actually when he started talking about his favorite baseball team...which stemmed from his favorite player...who happened to star in a movie he appeared in after his retirement...which was his favorite genre of movies.

Come to think of it, she may not have actually blacked out, but she sure as hell wished she had.

"Cool, I've seen a couple of those movies, but I'm more of the action hero versus just the straight action, like *Die Hard*," she said and immediately realized it was on his man-card shelf.

"I'm a fan of those natural-disaster movies too. Something with a lot of suspense and CGI," he said.

"Oh, like *The Day after Tomorrow*? That's a good one. Honestly, besides that older movie *Volcano*, I don't think I've seen any other type of natural-disaster movie."

"*The Day After Tomorrow* is a really good one. Wanna watch that one?" he said as he slid off the bed.

She realized that he was heading to his bookshelf to pull out the movie before she even answered, "Sure, that sounds good."

Not even ten minutes into the movie, he started to feel Stacey up. She pretended not to notice at first, but then he started to kiss her neck. She finally responded with a turn of her head so they could actually kiss.

He kept his mouth open, and every time she tried to shift her head or open her mouth so their lips would actually touch, he opened his mouth wider. She had to hold back her laugh each time their teeth clattered together because of his bass-mouth technique. She shifted, and his chin stubble rubbed a little deeper into her chin. She pulled away from the kiss and muttered that they were missing the best part of the movie.

Once the movie was over, she said her goodbyes before something other than her mouth hung with shame.

"I'll text you later, beautiful," he said as she walked down the sidewalk.

Halfway back to the city on her train ride, she had to refrain from gagging and calling Mary to tell her to have a drink ready by the time she got home.

* * *

Without a word to Mary, who sat entranced by *Wonder Woman* for the fifth time, Stacey walked into the apartment. She was about to drink the raspberry vodka straight from the bottle, but thought better of it, poured two shots into a glass, and downed it all in one gulp.

"I'm guessing things with the ABCs guy tonight didn't go as planned?" Mary asked. She hung her head over the back of the couch and gazed at Stacey's upside-down look of disgust and distress.

"It's like you were there with me to witness it," Stacey lamented.

Mary's mouth pinched down into a silent "yikes" expression. "So just how bad was it anyway?"

An image of his parents' faces as she walked in popped into Stacey's head, and she poured another shot into the glass.

Mary sprang up from the couch and pulled the glass out of Stacey's hand. "Slow down there, Sally. You already had one hump tonight; you don't need another." Mary started to cackle at her own joke, but it fizzled out as soon as she looked at Stacey's face.

"Is that look because I may have just called you a camel?" Mary asked softly.

With a raise of her eyebrow, Stacey shifted her weight to release some of the uncomfortable energy she'd created in the room, only to stumble back the smallest step. "Jesus, have *you* been drinking tonight? 'Cause, if so, I need to catch up to you in order to tell you about this debacle."

Two hours later, a full bottle of vodka gone, Stacey lay on her side on the living floor with a fistful of tissues and a near-comatose Mary on the couch.

"I thought I was going to feel better about myself after all of this, but I just don't see it happening. I thought it would be fine if I got what I wanted out of them and never talked to them again, but now I can see it doesn't mean anything. It needs to mean something!" Stacey slurred. She rolled onto her back, and her head fell to the side toward Mary.

Mary responded with a low snore.

Stacey felt a warm wave of anger wash over her, and her ears began to ring. "Glad to see I'll always get sympathy whenever I need it," Stacey said as she struggled to stand up.

Without turning off the light in the living room, she stumbled into the bedroom and fell asleep as soon as her head hit the pillow.

* * *

"You look like shit; I hope you know that," Lisa said as soon as Stacey walked into work the next morning.

"Oh my goodness, thank you so much for letting me know. I hadn't the foggiest," Stacey snapped.

Lisa leaned back, and her face for just a single moment showed that it had the capability to be genuinely surprised, but then it snapped back into its normal judgmental look. "Don't have to be a dick about it." Lisa swiveled back around toward her computer and effectively put an end to the conversation.

Stacey took a deep breath, preparing to respond, but saw Greg shaking his head, eyes wide, indicating caution. She released the breath with a sigh and heavily sat down in her chair.

* * *

After eight rough hours of a never-ending headache aided by the snapping and clicking of Lisa's gum and keyboard, respectively, Stacey found herself in a bar with Greg.

"Hate to be the bearer of lame news, but I'm not drinking," she said as they sat down at a high table near the back.

"Oh, ho, but here's the kicker: you are. Just have one drink, and you'll feel better."

"Doesn't that only work if it's the morning after, and you have a hangover?"

"Judging by how rough you looked all day, it doesn't really matter because you're still hungover as fu-uck," Greg said, dragging out the vowel for emphasis.

With a swish and a flick, Stacey gracefully flipped him the bird and resigned herself to ordering a vodka cranberry when the waitress made her way to their table.

"So I'm guessing this is from getting almost fired yesterday?" Greg asked.

Stacey took a long and procrastinating breath, but immediately regretted it because she could smell how long it had been since they properly cleaned the bar. "I'm not going to lie; it is. I mean, how can one person be such a jerk and try to get someone fired like that?"

"That's just the way Lisa is, and you've known her for as long as I have. You can't fix those types of personalities, no matter how hard you try. I'm pretty sure she wouldn't change even if she was working in retail or fast food where she was humiliated and learning how to be humble. Jesus, if she was ever on a diet of 'humble,' we could use her as a decoration at Halloween."

"You's right." Stacey nodded. She took a sip of the drink when it arrived, and her throat felt as if she had just taken a swig of really potent acid. A chuckle rumbled out of Greg, and it took everything in her power not to pour her drink on him.

"Don't even think about it," Greg said.

Stacey batted her eyelashes while she looked behind her dramatically. "Who, me? Whatever are you referring to?"

Greg just shook his head and threw back a gulp of his beer before he said, "Girls are so lucky that they can just bat their eyelashes and somehow everything is forgiven."

"It's a gift and a curse; it all depends on how often it's used, and how effective it is," she said with a shrug.

"Greg!" a man yelled in delighted surprise from the bar.

Stacey looked for the source of the gloriously deep voice and saw a Captain America look-alike, with his Dorito-shaped torso and the height to match. His wide smile revealed a subtle flaw in symmetry—a dimple on just one cheek.

"Jake!" Greg answered with just as much enthusiasm. He stood up, met the other man halfway, and proceeded to engage in what seemed to be an uncomfortable combination of a handshake and a hug.

All Stacey could think about was how weird it must be to have two arms squashed in between two bodies like that. She mentally shook her head to clear it as both men made their way back to the table.

"Hey, Stacey, this is Jake. He was my roommate for two years at college, and we were on the football team together. Jake, this is Stacey. We work together at *Econ-Living* magazine."

Jake shook her hand with a firm but gentle handshake, not one of those wimpy handshakes because he didn't want to hurt her "wittle" hand. Her train of thought started to derail while she focused on Jake's big yet soft hands, so much so that she almost didn't hear him ask how long Greg and she had known each other.

"About three years now. We started at the same time. Where do you work?"

"I'm actually an attorney at Yung and Wreckels. I'm here with a couple of coworkers. We just won a case that we had been working on for a while and needed to come out and celebrate. Wanna join us? I'm sure they won't mind having a couple of new people join us."

"We wouldn't want to bother you guys if you are celebrating—" Greg started to say, but Jake just clipped him on the shoulder.

"It'll be totally fine! Are you worried we're stiff because we're attorneys? We've been known to cut a rug." He laughed.

Stacey wanted to kick her heart for skipping a beat at the dumbest of times, and his use of such a stupid idiom happened to be one of those times. "I mean, if you guys are fine with that, I'm fine with it," Stacey said.

Greg polished off his beer in two gulps and nodded in agreement.

"This is Greg and Stacey. This is Dave, Sasha, Samantha, and Thomas," Jake announced once everyone had filtered over to their table.

Everyone said their hellos, and once they had the chance to explain that they were in family law, Dave offered to buy Stacey and Greg a drink.

"Maybe in a little bit if you're still offering. I'm slowly making my way through this one first," Stacey replied at the same time that Greg said, "Hey, thanks, man, I'll just take a beer if you're serious."

Dave let out a little chuckle and nodded as he placed an order for a pitcher.

"So what case win are you guys celebrating?" Stacey asked Jake, but quickly made eye contact with the others to appear more engaging.

Jake took in a rough breath and gave the back of his head a scratch, which caused his dress shirt to pull taut against his left bicep and pec. That meant Stacey was left to seem engaging to everyone, including Jake's muscles.

"It was a tough one, legally and emotionally. This isn't the first time we've had a case like this, but this one was the worst because of how intense it got. It was a custody battle between the mother and father of a four-year-old little girl. The mother is a substance abuser, and even with video evidence, the judge was still leaning toward the mother having custody because that's just how it goes. It finally took the mother being arrested during a drug deal, which she went to while high, mind you. The worst part was that she had her daughter with her.

"The trial from start to finish took a whole year, and now the girl is in kindergarten at a good school and living with the father who happens to be a teacher there. There are a lot more details to it, but I don't want to bore you with them," Jake said, mistaking Stacey's glazed look for zoning out.

"Oh no, you weren't boring me! It all sounds so sad, but I'm just glad that the girl is safe and with the good parent."

"Us too. We almost contemplated doing it pro bono, but due to how long it went on, we had to settle with only charging him for half of our services," Thomas said.

"That's so sweet of you! There goes my stereotype of lawyers being cold, ruthless ambulance chasers."

"Oh, you are right about that stereotype, but that's only for the injury lawyers. If we were all characters in *Parks and Recreation*, they would be Jamm. Those cheap attorneys they have at jails would be that sewer-plant guy," Sasha said.

Stacey cringed at the thought of how scummy lawyers had seemed before, and felt the smallest bit of disappointment to realize that they really could be sleazy.

"So what do you guys do?" Dave asked after they talked a little more about the law firm and how it only focused on family because of the great number of custody litigations and the high divorce rate in the city.

"We work at *Econ-Living* magazine," Greg said.

"Oh yeah! My sister reads it all the time because she loves the fact that you guys don't push the high-priced items for the decorating recommendations like all the other magazines do," Samantha said.

Stacey lit up a little to hear someone else had the same frustration. "Honestly, that was the main reason I wanted to work there. I was getting tired of seeing those one-hundred-dollar throw pillows in other magazines, and I wanted to be a part of what they represented."

"The name of the magazine is a little tacky, but it sells because it's catchy," Greg added.

They all nodded their agreement, and soon everyone started conversations among themselves.

"So do you like it at the magazine? What do you do there?" Jake asked Stacey, leaning toward her in anticipation of being able to hear her answer over the chatter.

"We're editors. We haven't quite made it to independent writers, but that's more Stacey's thing," Greg answered for her. His sentence gradually dropped in volume at the end, and a small hiccup bubbled up out of his throat.

Stacey flashed Greg a questioning eyebrow raise, but he simply replied with a shrug and a sip. "Yeah, my goal is to be a writer for them, or at least a writer in general. I went for English literature and feel like I need to do something with it," Stacey said.

"I get that. It took me a while to finally land on being an attorney, and once I figured it out, I had tunnel vision getting it done. Granted, sometimes it felt like I was mining the tunnel myself before I could see the light at the end."

"That's how I'm feeling right now! This is a fantastic job, but if they won't let me write, I might have to carve my way somewhere else," Stacey said.

Jake stepped closer to Stacey as he smiled in agreement and glanced over at Greg. "What about you? I haven't seen you in years. How have you been, man? Now that I know we are so close, we'll have to hang out again sometime."

"I've been good. I've been playing for a pickup lacrosse team that just plays with other pickup teams around the city, which keeps me in shape."

"But I thought you hated lacrosse."

"Because the college team was full of stoners, and I wasn't about that. I'm still not," Greg said.

Jake reached his fist out, and Greg gave it a limp bump. "They were some of the worst kids on campus. You know, their house was next to the one I lived in with Amy. They had some awesome parties, but they also blasted music pretty much every night, especially during finals week because they were all rec and leisure majors and didn't have any finals."

"Yo, how is Amy doing? You guys were really good together, so I'm actually a bit surprised to see that you don't have a ring on your finger."

"Yeah, about Amy. We broke up a year after graduation because she got an awesome job offer out in Seattle, and we realized the distance would be too much. It hurt, but it was amicable."

Greg placed a comforting hand on Jake's shoulder, and Jake simply thanked him with a cheers of his glass of beer.

"Are you guys still in touch at least? I feel like you could have at least been friends," Stacey asked.

"We still talk from time to time, and she actually got married last year to a software engineer at a tech company, which is technically not an HR violation." Jake chuckled.

"You weren't invited to the wedding, were you?" Greg asked with an anticipatory wince.

"No, and even if I was, I don't think I would have been able to get away from work for a wedding on the other side of the country. I don't think it would have been awkward or anything like that; it's just that being an adult can be really draining."

The other attorneys overheard Jake, and all raised their glasses in solidarity.

Stacey's skin started to prickle as she watched how easygoing, genuinely funny, and kind he was. For a moment, she had a hard time believing that he was an actual person and not someone practicing different personalities for an audition. She kept finding herself trapped by his single dimple when he smiled and the fact that he could probably cut glass with his jawline.

Suddenly Stacey realized Greg was standing next to her. The smell of leftover lasagna from lunch and his sixth beer draped over Stacey like a weighted blanket. "How are you feeling? Can I get you another drink? It looks like you were able to put that one back all right."

He wobbled for the smallest moment, and Stacey couldn't hide her smile. "I'm good. I feel like it's starting to get late, so I might head home soon anyway."

"How about you, good sir? How are you doing? You're just this side of turnt."

"I'm feeling fantastic, thanks for asking," he said with a contradictory tone.

Stacey raised an eyebrow in question and took his glass out of his hand. He started to protest, but she pushed it to the well side of the bar where he couldn't reach past her.

"I believe you, but I feel like you won't feel the same way in the morning if you keep this up. Come on; let's get you home because it *is* a work night."

She put a hand on his arm, and he gently covered it with his own. It was warm and familiar, and Stacey hated the fact that she thought that. With her other hand, she tapped Jake on the arm.

"I'm gonna take him home. It's been a long day, but it didn't take him long to throw back all of those pints."

"He used to be so good at holding his alcohol. I guess that's what old age will do to you."

"It was really nice meeting you, Jake, and it was really nice meeting everyone," she said as she looked around to the others to try to seem a bit more polite, "and I hope you enjoy the rest of your night."

"It was really nice meeting you too, Stacey. Hope to catch up with you again sometime. Do you live around here?"

"I don't, but this little keg lives, like, a block over, so thankfully I won't have to pay for a cab twice."

"Keg?" Jake asked confusedly.

"Because he's full of beer, and I'm tapping him out," Stacey said matter-of-factly.

A moment passed before Jake finally started to laugh. "That is hilarious and really clever. You don't mind if I take that from you, do you?"

"I'll have to talk to my intellectual-property attorney, and then we can talk," Stacey said after a beat.

Jake's eyes seemed to shimmer in delight, but Stacey chalked it up to the lights over the pool tables nearby. He gave a genuine laugh, turned to his coworkers, and repeated Stacey's retort, but he started laughing too hard to finish the second.

Dave started to join in first, and soon the other three chimed in. Thomas went in for a high five.

"We really need to hang out again, and hopefully I will remember to invite some of the intellectual-property lawyers from the other firm in our building. Are you sure you need to leave though?" Jake asked.

"I don't mean to be a party pooper, but I need to make sure he makes it home all right."

"That's all right. It's really cool that you're that nice. It was great meeting you, and hope you make it to your home all right," Jake said. Stacey brought her hand up for another shake, but he wrapped her in a one-arm hug instead.

With the final goodbyes said, Greg and Stacey were finally out in the loud and smoggy night, which was surprisingly refreshing after that subtle mold and stale, dirty beer smell of the bar. Greg was silent during the walk to his apartment building and only bumped into Stacey four times as he drunkenly staggered along. Once outside his door, he struggled with his keys and dropped them.

Stacey released an exasperated sigh, and in one fell swoop picked up the keys and unlocked the door. She directed Greg toward his bedroom in the dark and was annoyed when she heard the keys slip off the counter, to which she had evidently miscalculated the distance.

Greg tried to kick off his shoes without untying them, lost his balance, and tumbled to the floor. "Who the fuck put a carpet on the wall," he mumbled into the floor.

With the sigh of a girl who was starting to lose her patience, Stacey helped him get up and take the two steps to his bed, onto which he flopped heavily with a loud groan.

Stacey turned to leave, but heard a soft and deep "Wait." She sat down on the bed next to Greg and listened to his breathing start to deepen.

"Thanks for walking me home. You're a really fantastic woman. I hope you know that."

"I know. I know. I did my civic duty of not letting you stumble in front of a taxi."

"No, I'm serious. You are the most kindhearted, sweet, and funny girls I have ever met, and sometimes I just want to shake you when you look like you're starting to get down on yourself," he said.

Stacey sat stunned, staring at his shadowy silhouette backlit by the streetlight outside.

"Thank you. I know you're not as douchey as I originally thought, and I really like this gentle side of you," she said.

He rubbed her back, and she found herself lying down so he could spoon her. His familiar height, personal body heat, and gentle but protective arm draped over her quickly lulled her to sleep.

* * *

Stacey suddenly awoke in a pool of sweat and looked around the room in confusion, growing worried that the nightstand looked nothing like Mary's coffee table, and the wall didn't have the large abstract painting Mary's living room wall did. She blinked her eyes a few times to wipe out some of the grogginess so she could clearly see the numbers on the clock on the nightstand: 1:37 a.m. A wave of anxiety washed over her, but it ebbed to a low simmer just as quickly when her eyes landed on the hockey-player Pop Vinyl figure Stacey had given to Greg last year because they just happened to be each other's Secret Santa.

She rolled over to be confronted with Greg's shoulder blades and had to resist the urge to jetpack him. She rolled onto her back and debated on whether she should stay the night and go to work the next day, with just enough time to run home to change, or chance the subway at that time of night. Just as the late-night drowsiness started to take her over, she realized she could just Uber home.

* * *

Forget your mom, you're the one who's got it going on, a match named Peter messaged the next morning.

Stacey chuckled to herself, but almost choked on her cereal spoon in the process. She heard Mary opening and closing every drawer in her dresser before uttering a defeated sigh. The sound of footsteps approached Stacey.

"I can't find my gold sandals. They would have gone perfectly with this dress," Mary lamented. She poured some coffee into her travel mug and took a sip without adding anything.

Stacey dramatically grimaced, and Mary dramatically slurped in retaliation. "Would it be a bad time to remind you that you threw them out because the strap thing broke?"

"As long as it's not a bad time to ask where that little smile came from," Mary said as she sat across from Stacey at the kitchen table.

"No, but don't get disappointed that it's because someone just sent me a really clever pickup line, and I kinda want to go for it."

Mary stole Stacey's phone and looked for the recent message. She chuckled just as Stacey had.

"That is pretty clever. Is that seriously the first guy that referenced that song?"

"It is. And I'm honestly kind of salty that it took someone this long to say it. I mean, in this context. Fuck the kids I went to middle school with," Stacey said.

Mary started to sing the chorus of the song, and it took every ounce of Stacey's self-control not to throw the rest of the cereal at her.

"What are you going to say in response?"

"I'll go with the truth because it really is clever. And sometimes they actually respond well to sincerity," Stacey said and ignored the fake gagging Mary began doing.

"You feeling up to things after the Staten Island stallion you sucked face with last weekend?" Mary asked.

Stacey cringed at the thought of his parents being a couple of rooms away and at how toolish his movie collection was. "I mean, it wasn't as far as Staten Island. But I think I'm feeling better. I'm just going to have to be smarter about it and not just go because they are a letter on the list."

"But I thought that was the purpose," Mary said, genuinely confused.

"Part of it started that way, but the other part was for me to start growing in confidence and self-love, but I can't do that if I'm settling."

Mary shrugged, but nodded in understanding, and stood up with her mug. "Well, while you're thinking of a clever but honest response, Mama's gotta head to work, and judging by the time, I suggest you do the same."

Stacey looked at her phone for the time, bolted out of her seat, and ran to get her purse and things together while muttering the word "shit" with every footstep.

* * *

Stacey stepped off the elevator ten minutes late, but the only thing she thought about was how Greg would look at her for sneaking out on him in the middle of the night. She turned the corner toward her cubicle cluster and was relieved yet disappointed when she saw his empty desk chair.

"Good morning, Miss Tardy," Lisa said without looking up from her computer.

"Like you've never been late before."

"Can't recall." Lisa shrugged.

Stacey rolled her eyes and spun in her chair to boot her computer. She looked up and caught a glimpse of Greg wandering toward her with a mug in hand.

"Nice of you to show up," Greg joked as he passed her. Their eyes connected for a moment, and for a split second she swore she saw a glint of pain in his eyes.

Well, fuck. Stacey scolded herself for being a terrible person.

"That's what I already told her," Lisa pitched in.

"There was some traffic on the way in. Plus, I may have made a pit stop in the bathroom when I remembered I'd have to see Lisa's face," Stacey said.

Greg chuckled before he could hide his mouth.

"Oh, that's very original. I think you may have thrown up the possibility of being funny."

"Jesus, just fuck her already! You do realize all this pent-up anger is because you're frustrated about something else, right?" Greg asked from his desk.

"I'm sure she hasn't been touched since her breakup, so I suspect she would like that a little too much."

"Calling me undesirable, that's very original," Stacey echoed.

Lisa huffed and focused on her computer to tune them out.

Stacey smiled at Greg, and they raised their hands for an air high five over Lisa's head.

* * *

So what's something you like to do on the weekend? Peter messaged Stacey while she was on her lunch break.

It depends on the week I had, if it was a chill week, I'll go out to the bars. If it was crazy, I like to re-coop and stay in. What about you?

I have a season pass to Jones Beach so I'm usually there on the weekends, even if it's a cover band or some classic rock band full of the original geriatrics

Stacey was thrown off for a moment by his crudeness, but she didn't let herself linger on it too long.

I try to go at least once a month because they tend to get some pretty cool people to play there, Stacey lied. The last time she went to Jones Beach was to see some local boy, who had made it big, because he was the only good thing to go through there that summer.

"How's the book coming?" Greg materialized beside her on the bench in the courtyard.

Startled, Stacey jumped and almost fell off the bench. After she recovered, she punched him on the arm.

"That's assault. How about I get one of those Mounties over here to report you?" Greg said.

She looked over his shoulder, and there were in fact three policemen on horses at the other end of the courtyard. "I thought they only hung around Times Square," Stacey mused aloud.

"Don't change the subject. Who you messagin'?" Greg asked before taking a bite of his hot dog. He was watching Stacey a bit more intensely than she felt comfortable with.

"Some guy I matched with on Tinder," she said. Greg's shoulders hunched a little bit, so she rushed to add, "I'm only talking to him because he's the first one to have a cute pickup line based around the song."

"Which song?"

"You know, the pick song about the guy crushing on his neighbor's mom."

"Jesus, I forgot about that song. That takes me back to middle school…in a good way because middle school sucked for me," Greg said after taking another bite.

Stacey humorlessly laughed loudly. "I know you mentioned it before, but I just can't imagine you having a hard time in middle school. I don't believe it. I bet you were the football jock that worked out with his older brother because *he* was working out to stay the football jock of the high school."

"I played, but I wasn't serious about it until high school. But it really was hard. I hadn't grown yet, so I was actually shorter than the other boys, and then I had braces from the day I started sixth grade to the day I finished eighth."

"Well, that's an oddly specific and unnecessarily cruel timeline," Stacey sympathized.

Greg simply gave a limp shrug of his shoulders and took another bite.

She looked back down at her phone and absently looked at the time. When the air between them grew silent, she decided to fill the silence. "He seems nice at least. But that's not all I'm looking for," Stacey said with a suggestive eyebrow wiggle as if on autopilot. She suddenly realized that, instead of to a girlfriend, she was talking to Greg, the guy she had hooked up with, about whom she was confused—why had she wanted to stay the whole night to just cuddle with him?—the guy who had once treated her as just another "girl" friend over the years of working together.

Greg looked up at Stacey, first in confusion, and then with crushing devastation—she was already looking back down at her phone. Her eyes were glued on the flashing typing bubble as the phone gave a short *brrt* as the message finally came in.

When it comes to concerts, the best thing to do is have fun, honestly. And I have fun all the time and I think that's what gets me so excited for the next one.

"Like this, he seems pretty chill and not awkward with the first couple of exchanges. You know how it goes; there's always that weird set of obligatory volleys you throw at one another before the conversation can actually start. And I don't think that's going to happen," Stacey babbled to try to erase her previous innuendo.

Greg stared her down for a couple of slow chews, a long swallow, and a sigh before he got up and wiped his hands on his pants. "I gotta get going. I clocked out a lot sooner than I intended and need to clock back in before HR has an aneurysm." Before Stacey had time to reply with a farewell, he had already made his way toward the building.

She sat still for five minutes, simply staring at the front door, but inside she was torn between being annoyed by his reaction and being worried that she may have hurt or insulted him in some way.

CHAPTER
13

Mary: *Do you think he may have gone to the wrong Starbucks?*

Stacey: *It's New York fucking City, I wouldn't be surprised*

She sat at a table near the front of the coffee shop a few days later, having agreed to meet Peter after many topics of conversation. The more she messaged him, the more insistent he got about meeting in person. It got to the point that she simply submitted to meeting him...in a public place...that she frequented, so the employees would recognize her.

As Mary's typing ellipses popped up, a tall gentleman walked into the coffee shop and looked around as if searching for something. Stacey recognized, of all things, his buzz-to-fade hairstyle, and she waved him over. His face lit up once his eyes met hers, and the smallest of flushes washed over her.

"Hey, Stacey," he said with the hint of a question when he made it to the table.

"Hey, Peter, nice to meet you. Did you wanna order something real quick?"

"Sure."

He ordered a barely-any-coffee, blended frozen drink because he didn't like coffee, she ordered a venti caramel latte, and they settled back in at the table Stacey had secured.

"Sorry I'm late. I didn't realize how far of a walk it was," he said.

"You walked here?"

"Oh yeah! I live a few blocks down and over, so I figured it would be easiest just to walk."

"This is a pretty central area. How's it living here?"

"It's definitely pricey, but thankfully my parents are cool about helping me out if I need it."

"Oh? Where do they live?"

"They live over in Hempstead, but we're still pretty close."

"What do you do for work?" Stacey asked, trying not to be too obvious about already not enjoying the date.

"I work for a restaurant as a dishwasher and busboy when it gets too busy for the servers to clean up."

Stacey nodded her head in forced amusement and smiled to hide how annoyed she was getting with herself for going on dates with oversized children. But they started getting into a rhythm of conversation, and she was able to coax herself into enjoying it for a bit…until he got back to the conversation about concerts. He arrogantly mentioned he had been to a concert every other weekend for the past three months, both in the city and upstate, how two of the concerts were artists he had already seen, and how he had a season pass to the Jones Beach theatre. Stacey mentally calculated how much a ticket would cost, even with a season pass, calculated how much he *wasn't* making as a *dishwasher*, and tried to figure out where he was getting all the money.

"Do you like country music?" he asked.

She bashfully shook her head and knew what was ahead, but not how much.

"How do you not like country? It's America's music, and it's always classic. It doesn't matter if it's Wille Nelson or Dierks Bentley; it's such a great genre. Have you even listened to country before?"

"I mean, yeah, because that's how I know I don't like it."

He brushed that off with a condescending comment and suddenly shifted to talking about his ex, who was also not a fan of country. "She was a psycho. I can't even tell you how crazy she was. There was a point where she wasn't taking her birth control pills and insisted on using condoms that she had or brought over, and once I found out it was because she was poking holes in them. I broke up with her. She was obsessed with having a kid with me. I'm not ready for kids, and I don't know if I even want kids."

"I'm with you there. I'm in a weird place where I can barely take care of myself. I don't know if I'm ready for kids."

During the ten more minutes of conversation, topics switched faster than she was able to keep up with—more of the ex; high school interests; the reason he wasn't a licensed driver, even though he'd grown up on Long Island, not in the city; playing hockey at local rinks when he had the chance.

As Stacey began to tear apart the cup's hot sleeve because she had finished her latte fifteen minutes before, and after he took the last ice-clumped sip of his drink, he gave her a wide smile. "When would you be able to go on a second date? I get a discount at the restaurant I work at, so we can always go there. They have really good tortellini that you just have to try. I can't wait.

"I also can't wait for you to meet my parents, so they can see who I'm dating now," he said with a sheepish smile.

Stacey's breath caught in her throat; she was thrown back by his comments and completely unable to form a direct response to them. She decided to deflect with an obvious look at her phone for the time. "We can figure it out soon. But I think I should get going. I live a couple of train rides away, and I have to work in the morning."

"Yeah, we can figure out where to go for our next date. And I get that; sometimes I have to wake up early to go to work."

They walked out of the coffee shop together, and just as they were about to part ways, he leaned over and planted a quick kiss on her cheek. She had a hard time focusing between the kiss itself and the indignation that burned inside her because his giant nose was pressed up against her cheek harder than his lips were.

Once she muttered a forced compliment and bid him goodbye once more, they turned and finally did part ways. She kept glancing over her shoulder to make sure that he wasn't following her.

* * *

The moment she made it into Mary's apartment, she grabbed a can of spiked seltzer from the fridge and sat down at the dining table across from Mary. Mary looked up from her meat-lovers' sub and raised a brow at Stacey, who got more than halfway through the can before Mary finally swallowed her bite and wiped the mayo off the side of her mouth.

"I'm guessing it went just as you thought it would."

"A little worse actually, but that's putting it lightly."

Mary winced in response and took another bite out of her sub. Through the bread and the turkey, she asked, "What was the worst part?"

"All of it, honestly, but I ended it a lot sooner than he seemed to have wanted to. Did you know that he wanted to introduce me to his parents because he wanted to show them who he was dating?" Stacey huffed.

Mary did a small spit take with her Sprite before she sputtered, "I'm sorry. He said what?"

"Yeah! And then as we were leaving, he gave me a kiss, but I barely felt it because his nose dug into my cheekbone."

"Bro, never kiss on the first date. And he had the nerve to say you guys were dating?"

"Oh yeah! And he spent half of it going off about how his ex was a psycho and how he goes to so many fucking concerts. It came off as condescending, honestly."

Stacey finished the can and grabbed another one from the fridge. As she made a mental inventory of how many were left, she thought about getting more peach liqueur and malted teas, to mix together, the next time they made it to the liquor store. She took a few more sips as she walked over to the couch and flopped down right in the middle.

"I don't know if I want to do this list anymore, especially if this is all that this great city has to offer. Even though we didn't fuck, can I add him to the list?"

"It's your list; you can change the rules of who goes on it as you see fit."

Stacey paused a moment to ponder and then leaned toward the coffee table to grab the list and a pen. She wrote "Peter" as best she could with her chicken-scratch penmanship.

"He may not have fucked me physically, but, man, did he fuck me mentally."

* * *

Luke: *Have you been to McGil's on 3rd down in Lenox Hill? They have a really good wing sauce if you like it spicy or else I'd recommend the Cuban*

An odd giddiness flushed through Stacey when the message came in. It had only been a week since they first started talking, but she was thoroughly enjoying how responsive he was to her messages, how he didn't seem to let the conversation fizzle out, and how he actually initiated a new topic if one was naturally coming to a close. So far, it had been one of the most engaging interactions she had had with someone from that godforsaken app.

She didn't want to think about the fact that it was actually more of a rebound of sorts in order to combat the taste, literally and figuratively, of Peter from her memory.

She texted Luke, *I have a couple of times and am actually a big fan of their garlic parm fries*

A woman of good taste, those fries are out of this world, he quickly replied.

Stacey had to hold in the blush as she set the phone down to continue proofreading an article on decor hacks using napkin holders sold at a dollar store.

"How are you not done with that article yet?" Lisa asked next to her. "Oh, I know; it's because you've been on your phone nonstop since you walked in."

Stacey closed her eyes as she breathed in, one…two, and breathed out, one…two, before turning toward Lisa's smug face. "There isn't a policy against cell-phone use as long as we are getting through our workload for the day, and I'm making good time so far.

"How do you always have something to say to me? Oh, I know; it's because you have nothing better to do with your boring life."

Lisa whipped around as soon as she heard Greg snort from behind her. Stacey peeked around to see his shoulders bouncing with silent chuckles.

"Laugh it up. And I do have something better to do with my life because I know Steve has had his eye on me for a promotion. It can't come soon enough because I don't know how much longer I—" Lisa said, only to be cut off as Stacey held up her index finger in the universal "one moment, please" as she read the latest message from Luke.

She looked up to see a seething Lisa sucking on her teeth. "What were you saying, hon?" Stacey said.

Lisa opted for huffing and rolling her eyes, instead of continuing her monologue, and then she turned back to her computer.

"Good talk," Stacey muttered under her breath.

As soon as the clock struck 5:05 p.m., and everyone else had made their way to the elevator, Stacey finally clocked out and began rummaging through her purse for her emergency makeup. All that she was able to procure was a nude lip gloss, which was more tacky than glossy, and that tried-and-true, pink-and-green tube of purse-use-only mascara. She opened the camera in her phone to watch herself put on the mascara and nearly missed jamming the wand into her eye when she saw Greg walking up behind her on the screen. "You need a cowbell or something; you scared the shit out of me!"

"Sorry," he muttered before sitting on the edge of Lisa's desk to face her.

"Just don't get into the habit of doing that. I could have gotten you on eye-surgery charges. Imagine if I needed to wear an eye patch around the office. Steve might finally get off my back, but that's about the only good thing about it," she rambled.

When she switched hands to start on her other eye, she sensed that Greg was still watching her. "Yes?"

"I was gonna ask if you wanted to get some drinks tonight, but it looks like you might already have plans. It's darts night at my bar, and those guys are a riot."

"There would go my other eye. Call me Ralphie!" she joked. She was slightly concerned about Greg's blank expression; it was as if his hard drive had just beeped, and his desktop flashed to the blue screen of death.

"You know, the line from *A Christmas Story*. 'You'll shoot your eye out, kid!'" Stacey mimed in a crotchety, old voice.

Greg shifted his gaze around the room as if embarrassed to make further eye contact.

As calmly as she could, Stacey placed the mascara wand back in the tube, screwed it shut, and tossed it into her purse. "Do not tell me you have never seen *A Christmas Story*." Stacey counted on her fingers as she quoted, "'Drink your Ovaltine,' 'Fra-gee-lay, sounds Italian,' 'I triple-dog dare you'?" She was starting to become viscerally upset and personally offended, as if Greg were starting to mock her, even though his face never changed once. "They literally played it for twenty-four hours straight on one of the TV stations years ago. I don't know if they still do."

"You can say whatever you want, but I have never actually seen it. It just looked so stupid, so that's why I never watched it," Greg said.

"That's the whole point! That's it; we aren't friends anymore. Have fun losing an eye at darts tonight, bucko!" Stacey said as she whipped her purse over her shoulder.

"At least now I know where your childish humor comes in," Greg said. He followed her to the elevators and pressed the Down button before she could.

"You seriously haven't seen that movie? Let me guess; you were watching *It's a Wonderful Life* like a pretentious tool."

"Actually, it was *National Lampoon's Christmas Vacation*," he said.

"But the movie *I* watched was the stupid one. Got it. Take a shot for me to wash down that double standard, will ya?"

Greg chuckled lightly as he held the door open for Stacey to step off first.

"Only if you have a drink knowing that you missed out on the best Christmas movie ever."

"Honestly, I'll take a drink just because you didn't say *Die Hard* was a Christmas movie. If I have to hear one more dude bro try to argue that just because it takes place at Christmas, I'll start saying *A Cinderella Story* is a sports movie just because it has football games in it."

"Keep going. I actually kind of want to hear that argument," Greg said mockingly.

She stuck a middle finger up as she looked at the clock on her phone and muttered a soft "shit."

"Rain check, or else I'm going to be late to free garlic-parm fries."

"I KNEW IT! Girls are only going on dates to get free food."

"Good night, Greg," Stacey said exasperatedly.

* * *

She made it to McGil's with two minutes to spare. She leaned up against the bar and realized a moment too late that the man on the stool next to her was Luke.

"I was just about to message you to let you know it'll be a second before we can get an actual table," Luke said.

"It is kind of busy for a Wednesday night. I wonder what's going on."

"Oh, it's always like this. I actually work right around the corner from here and come here from time to time. I guess the twenty beers on tap really do something to all of the local stockbrokers."

"I thought cocaine was more their speed," Stacey joked. A flush of embarrassment washed over her as Luke's face puckered in confusion. "You know, like *The Wolf of Wall Street.*"

As soon as it left her mouth, his face lit up in recognition, and he laughed softly. "That's right! It's been a while since I've seen it."

Phew, I'm not zero for two, she thought in relief.

Luke's eyes lit up as he looked over Stacey's shoulders, and he stood up from the barstool. "Looks like our table is ready," he said. He let her precede him in following the hostess to a table a couple of rows away from the bar.

"The waitress will be with you shortly."

A pint of beer and cocktail later, they barely gave themselves time to think about the wait for their appetizers as they slowly started to lean towards one another, engrossed in their conversation.

"What do you mean it was a standard, boring classic novel? Did you not pick up on how sassy Ishmael is? For a novel written in the 1800s, it could have put some of us millennials and our love for dad jokes to shame."

"What on earth can you possibly be talking about? It's about sailing, a whale, and a way-too-extensive diary on blubber."

"Ah, but you are wrong, my good sir. Do you have any idea how hard I laughed when I read the scene when they were in the inn, having dinner, and the barkeep was, like, 'Would you like the clam chowder?' And Ishmael was, like, 'Only if it has more than one clam in it; I'm really hungry.' I will petition for that to be deemed the first official dad joke in written history," Stacey finished, slamming her fist on the table as if it held a gavel in a courtroom.

"Puh-lease, you know the Greeks, right? They were some freaks, so I would place my bets on there being some gems hidden away in the *Iliad*."

"Okay, bet. But I'll be here waiting for my twenty dollars when you can't find anything."

"Hate to say it, but I won't have to wait long to get the twenty dollars I deserve. Picture it: The scene with the

Cyclops, he's blinded by Odysseus, and when the Cyclops asked who he was, Odysseus said his name was Nobody. So when the Cyclops ran out to all of the other ones, and they asked who blinded him, he was, like, 'Nobody blinded me!'" Luke said proudly with his hand out to accept his reward.

"Damn it. But I declare that you only get fifteen dollars."

Luke looked wounded and almost offended at this. "And why is that?"

"Because that was actually from the *Odyssey*, so you get a penalty."

"I'll admit defeat, but just this one time," Luke said.

They had fallen into an easy, lighthearted round of chuckles when his phone started ringing, vibrating a quick staccato from the end of the table where he'd left it. Luke glanced at it, and a figurative "punch" of whiplash washed over her when his face seemed to drain of all color. He quickly sent the caller to voicemail before setting the phone back on the table, face down.

Luke looked around the bar and behind Stacey; he glanced at the wall of windows a row of tables over. She wasn't sure what he was looking for, but she started to get a gnawing shiver up her back. She suspected that she should be worried, not by his reaction, but by what caused it.

Before Stacey could sleuth out what it could have been, the waitress dropped the plate of loaded garlic-parm fries in front of them. "Are you guys ready to put in a dinner order now?" she asked cheerfully.

"Are you sure this is an appetizer because it looks to be the size of a meal itself," Stacey joked. She asked Luke what his thoughts were on his selected entrée, but he just gave her an absentminded nod of the head as he glanced between his phone and the windows.

With no response from either of them, before returning to the bar, the waitress awkwardly said she'd be back to check on them in a minute to see if they would be ready to order then.

"I forgot how big of a portion this was," Stacey said.

Luke took one bite at the same time as she did; he was just about to grab a second fry when his phone started buzzing again. It stopped faster than before, as if it was only a text message. Outwardly, it seemed as if he hadn't noticed, but Stacey saw his eyes flicker over to the phone between chews.

For a third time, his phone went off, and it kept buzzing. He raised his phone and read the screen, only to drop his jaw. His eyes frantically searched the bar and the other tables, and once they seemed to have landed on what he was looking for, he quickly scrambled to push his chair away from the table and stood up.

"What's going on; are you all right? What's wrong?" Stacey asked in a jumble of confusion and concern.

Luke's mouth gaped as he floundered to find the right words to say. "Funny, not-so-funny story. My wife's friend saw me here and told my wife."

Stacey froze in her seat on the first "wife," and her ears started to ring in indignation on the second "wife."

"You're what?" she bit out.

"Shit, I didn't mean for this to happen like this."

Like this? I feel like something like this shouldn't have happened in the first place, Stacey wanted to say as her blood boiled through her veins. But the shock closed her throat around her words.

Luke barreled on under Stacey's scrutinizing glare, "Look, you're actually really nice, and I got caught up in the connection we had. I was going to come clean to you soon."

"I can't believe this," Stacey finally said. She pushed her chair back and started to stand, but he held his palms out to stop her.

"No, please, don't go. I'm the one that needs to leave. I'll pay on the way out and add another drink for you. Please, it's the least I can do," he said as he started to back away, looking over her shoulder, toward what Stacey assumed was the spot where the wife's friend was.

She wasn't sure how to feel as she watched him throw on the bar a few more twenty-dollar bills than she thought were needed for the meal. After a couple of words to the bartender, he ran out.

She saw the bartender stare down at the pile of money before looking back at where Luke had pointed. She could see his brain working overtime as he tried to process what had just been said to him; then he took the money and walked toward the register.

Stacey shifted her eyes back to her drink, and she watched a couple of condensation drops race one another down the glass. Her shoulders fell forward, as if all her strength had oozed out of her as quickly as that condensation on the glass. She suddenly wanted to make herself smaller as she thought about the fact that the woman he was so scared to see could be, at that very moment, staring at Stacey, judging her, pitying her.

All the while, she never noticed the bartender wave her waitress over and exchange a couple of words, spreading the horror of what just happened at table twelve.

She didn't even notice when two tall men walked up to her table and took fries from her plate. It was on the second fry that she realized that the pressure she was feeling wasn't from humiliation, but was instead from trying to process what someone was trying to say to her.

"Helllooo? I said, how have you not touched any of these yet? I would have inhaled these in a second," a seemingly disembodied deep voice said as some spirits lifted it like a marionette.

She looked up and saw Greg staring down at her. She took a surprised breath, and the all-too-familiar scent of alcohol breath snapped her out of her paralyzed stasis. "Holy shit! I didn't see you come in."

"You all right? Is this actually a bad time?" the other man said.

She looked at the man who sat in the seat diagonally from her, and her brain flashed the Apple "Rainbow Wheel of Death" as she processed who it was. "Jake! Oh, um, I... Well, you see, it's..." she stammered. She finally settled on the tried-and-true "I've been better," punctuated with a shoulder shrug.

Greg raised an eyebrow as he went in for a couple more fries. Through the mouthful of potatoes, parmigiano, and oregano, he asked, "So what, might I ask, happened?"

Stacey hesitated for a second and looked down at her glass to watch an ice cube shift as it melted. She watched a once-trapped air bubble ride to the surface as she figured out how to describe what happened ten seconds before. "I don't know how you guys didn't see it. He literally just left," she finally said.

"I don't know; that drink seems pretty watered down, and the fries aren't as hot as they could have been, so something tells me it's been a hot minute since he left," Greg stated.

"Why don't we get you a new drink, huh?" Jake said from his side of the table.

Stacey absentmindedly nodded her head and looked up to try to find her waitress.

"How's everything over here; doing all right?" she asked. She seemed a bit more chipper than before, and Stacey couldn't help but feel it was because she was pitying her.

"I'll have another drink."

"Are you good on the fries for now, or would you like something else?"

"Just the fries for now," Stacey said.

"Not for long, he's gonna polish all of them off before you even have the chance to reach out for some," Jake said.

The waitress chuckled and turned her attention to Jake and Greg. "I'm guessing you'll be here for a little bit. What can I get for you two?"

"Whatever's Canadian you have on draught for both of us. Stacey, what would you like to eat?" Jake asked.

She glanced up and made the mistake of locking eyes on the concerned and caring look he gave her.

"How about the supreme pizza to share? How's that sound?" Greg asked, looking toward Stacey for her reaction.

"No olives or mushrooms," Stacey muttered.

The waitress slowly spoke as she wrote the order on her slip before giving a final nod and heading off to the bar.

"Spill," Greg said.

Stacey gave him a once-over with a raised eyebrow before asking, "How were the guys at dart night?"

"Don't change the subject, woman!"

"Well, since you asked so nicely, I found out he was married," she said. She shoved a couple of fries in her mouth and watched their expressions as she chewed. She couldn't help but get a small sense of enjoyment out of their abhorrence once they processed what she said.

"Yeah, that's gonna make for a two-more-drinks kind of night."

* * *

Two hours later, they were laughing so hard they were worried they were going to be kicked out of the restaurant. Movement caught the corner of Stacey's eye, and she saw Mary and Krista walk in and over to the bar.

"Hate to break up this giggle fest, but my ride's here," Stacey said. She tried to make eye contact with the waitress, but a fit of hiccups blurred her vision every ten seconds.

Greg's face pinched in confusion, and Jake's face looked as if a cab had pulled up right next to the table. He seemed to have realized too late how absurd that thought was and chuckled to himself.

Stacey felt a giddiness at how pure and genuine that whole display was. But her mood was crushed when she looked over at Greg.

"What do you mean your ride is here? Did you order an Uber when we weren't looking?"

"You have any idea how much an Uber is around these parts? No, Mary and Krista are here to walk me home."

Right then, Mary and Krista looked over as if they had heard her, and she gave them a little wave.

CHAPTER
14

"It is hot as balls today. I could really use a beach day," Mary rasped.

The AC in the building had stopped working the day before, and maintenance had yet to make it there to fix it. Stacey lay on the hardwood floor, while Mary melted on the couch Salvador Dalí-style, even though every window in the apartment was open, and they each had their own oscillating fan directed toward them.

"If I knew for sure I wouldn't lose skin to this floor when I got up, I would start packing a bag. Where would we even go?"

"Up to the Bronx maybe? Unless you know someone who's got a car that can take us to Long Island."

"Fuck, it'll be packed," Stacey groaned.

"All I need is enough space in the water for me to get wet; that is all I ask."

"All right, all right. Let me snail trail to my stuff so I can get ready." Stacey slowly pulled herself up and looked down to see a human-shaped sweat mark below her.

"You weren't fucking kidding with that snail trailing, were you?" Mary asked as she wandered into her bedroom.

* * *

An hour and an even hotter-than-hell subway ride later—complete with the smell from a tuna sub someone had left somewhere in the train car—they kicked off their flip-flops and made their way to the water.

"Told you it would be packed."

Within yards of the boardwalk, they had to dodge Hawaiian-shirt-clad sugar daddies and their silicone-filled sugar babies, various games of keep-it-up volleyball, and kids playing tag, before they found a decent spot near the water that felt comfortable enough to leave their stuff. Stacey peeled off her tank top and shorts to reveal a light-pink, off-the-shoulder, high-waisted two-piece, while Mary shrugged off her shorts to reveal the matching yellow-striped bottoms to the bikini top she'd worn there. Once the smell of Coppertone took over the smell of the middle-aged, beer-bellied man in the lounger next to them, they made their way to the water.

Mary dove right in as soon as the water level was up to her hips. "I feel like a completely new person, invincible almost."

"Cool your jets. Wait until you properly cool yourself off first before you go off saving the world," Stacey said. She walked into the water a little farther, and when the water level was up to her chest, she submerged herself. When she came back up, her hair curtained in front of her face, and she cursed herself for not pulling it back and securing it beforehand. She looked over at Mary and said, "I stand corrected. I'll be your sidekick."

"Hell yeah, that's the spirit!"

They stayed out in the water for a few more minutes, watching kids trying to surf in their inner tubes or getting dunked by their bigger siblings, before they wandered back out of the water to their stuff.

Just as Stacey was about to pull one of her towels out of the bag, a volleyball landed right next to her, spraying her legs with a fresh coat of sand. As she bent to pick it up, a man came over profusely apologizing for almost taking her out.

"It's okay. No harm, no foul," she said. She looked up to get a proper look and saw he had an abs four-pack, a nose ring, and a full sleeve of tattoos. With a mental sigh of appreciation, she handed the ball back to him. "Just means you'll have to work on getting it up," she said.

A wave of utter embarrassment washed over her, evaporating any water that might have still been on her body. He paused a moment, but to her surprise, he chuckled and seemed to let his hand purposely graze her fingers as the ball exchanged hands.

"Sounds like you know a thing or two about that. Thanks for the tip," he said. Even though he was wearing sunglasses, she could have sworn he winked at her.

Out of the corner of Stacey's eye, while she watched the man run back to his group, she saw Mary drop her own sunglasses down the bridge of her nose, a not-so subtle surprised expression on her face.

"Honestly, I didn't know you had it in you while sober," Mary said.

"Honestly, same. I don't know where that came from, but I was panicking that it was a really stupid thing to say."

They laid out their towels and flipped over twice before they started to shrivel and had to head back out to the water. When they returned to their spot on the beach the second time, the same guy came over with a duffel bag over his shoulder.

"What's your name?" he asked.

Her throat went dry for a moment, but she was able to spit out, "Stacey."

"I'm Travis. I'd like to see more of you sometime soon, maybe get some more tips. Is it cool if I have your number?"

In a haze, Stacey added her number to his phone and barely felt the buzz of his confirmation text before he left.

Just as he was out of earshot, Mary grabbed her arm and squealed. "Holy shit! Look at you! And who said you can't get a number without the help of apps these days," she said excitedly.

"You, if memory serves me right," Stacey retorted.

"Tomato, tomahto. And if things work out, that's another letter on your list."

"The list would have nothin' to do with seeing him again, if ya know what I mean."

* * *

So how many tattoos do you actually have? Stacey texted Travis, the beach hottie, later that night.

She wiped the sweat that had accumulated on her hand onto the throw pillow beside her while she waited for his reply. It wouldn't have done much to have wiped it on her sports bra or on her high school days' cotton shorts, so the pillow had to do for now.

Mary walked over and dropped a bowl of ice cream in front of Stacey before opting for a seat on the hardwood. "I'm going to sue this place if they don't get that AC fixed as soon as I wake up tomorrow," she said before digging into her mint chocolate chip.

Stacey sent another quick text before digging into her own bowl.

"What's Travis saying? Does he have a working AC, because I might have to join you if you end up going over to his place."

"He does, but he's still with his friends, so I'll have to suffer here with you. But, know, I would have kept going down to Queens if I had the fucking chance."

"Ew, Queens? Girl, have some pride in yourself."

"If I had seen more Levittown guys on this godforsaken app, you bet your tiny ass I would have hopped on that chance as soon as possible." Stacey pointed her spoon down at Mary as she spoke before taking another bite.

Mary's jaw dropped, and her hand flew to her chest as she let out a couple of dramatic huffs. "Excuse me, madam, but I'll have you know the correct term is *petite*, and a lot of other femmes really enjoy it," she defended, adding a heavy French accent to the word "petite."

"But, seriously, have you guys talked about anything juicy?"

"Not really, his messages are few and far between, so it's kinda hard to even remember what conversation we were having in the first place," Stacey said defeatedly.

"Well, you said he was with friends, didn't you? Maybe he doesn't want to seem rude to them. But the fact that he's messaging back still shows interest," Mary said hopefully.

Stacey gave a noncommittal shrug, winced at the sting from the light sunburn she had acquired at the beach, and set her phone down to focus on her ice cream, which was turning more into milk with every passing second. Just as she was slurping back her last spoon of chocolate chips, her phone buzzed on the coffee table.

"See? He wouldn't be texting you back if he wasn't interested," Mary said triumphantly.

I have two on my back and my sleeve I count as four because it took four sessions to get it done, Travis replied.

Her eyebrows furrowed for a moment while she tried to think of something to respond to that rather-dry message.

"What's that look for?"

"I don't know what to say next. I feel like it would have been normal to say what the tattoos were so it would be easier to lead to more conversation."

"Well, the vagueness helps you though. You can ask him what they are and which is his favorite. Boom, more conversation," Mary said to lighten the situation.

"I guess. I just feel like guys normally would have gone into detail with something like this."

"Girl, you are overthinking it. He's into you, so just go for it!"

CHAPTER
15

Stacey walked into work the next morning with stiff shoulders, a persistent sweat stain, and a kink in her neck. But when the blast of AC air brushed her cheeks as the elevator doors opened on her floor, she almost shed a tear.

"You look exceptionally blissful to be here today," Greg said as he rolled his chair over to her desk.

"If you were slowly being roasted alive for the last two days because your building's AC went out, you'd understand."

"I thought you were looking a little crispy on the edges," he said with a head-bob gesture toward her exposed shoulders.

"Oh that? That was thanks to the Bronx Riviera. Mary and I went out that way yesterday to try to escape our oven of an apartment. Who knew you needed to reapply sunscreen after *every time* you went into the water?" She gave herself a forehead tap with the heel of her palm.

"Ten out of ten dermatologists," Greg deadpanned.

Stacey returned with a quick middle finger.

He grabbed his heart as if he'd been shot. "You wound me with your love. Call me a masochist."

She rolled her eyes and turned toward her screen, but paid close attention to the fact that he stayed like that for five seconds before he rolled back over to his own desk.

* * *

"Monday happy hour?" Greg asked just as Stacey clocked out of her computer.

"I am always down for a drink. Your normal bar tonight?"

"Of course. The bartenders know my drink of choice, so it's always nice to have the pint ready for me at the end of the bar before I wander over to my usual table."

"Don't mean to be that guy, but that sounds like the beginning of a problem."

"Shut up, and grab a drink with me."

Twenty minutes later, they were walking down the steps into the basement bar, and just as he said would happen, there was a pint of beer sitting at the far end of the bar, which he grabbed on his way over to a table to the side of the bar.

"God, I hate you." Stacey chuckled while she waited for her own double vodka cranberry. "So how long have you been coming to this bar then?" Stacey asked as she sat down across from Greg.

"Since I moved into my current place, so two years? I stumbled upon it on a walk back from work one night, and I guess you could say the rest is history." He weaved his hands into a hammock behind his head and leaned back just slightly, but she could tell he was not-so-subtly flexing while he did so.

In response, she rolled her eyes, not so subtly, and took a sip from her glass. As she went to set it down, she noticed Greg's eyes focus on something at the front door behind her, and his demeanor shifted to what she could only describe as annoyance as he brought his arms down suddenly. As his hands passed over his face, Greg's expression changed, like a magician's trick, and he got up out of his chair.

"Jake! Didn't think I'd see you here on a Monday. How the fuck are ya?" He went in for that weird dude-bro handshake-hug thing.

Seriously, how is that not uncomfortable, Stacey asked herself. But her worry and confusion quickly dissipated and morphed into infatuation when she was reminded of that little dimple.

"Stacey, hi! It's so good to see you again. How have you been?" Jake gushed in genuine excitement.

A blush crept from Stacey's neck to her cheeks as she responded, "I've been really good! It's really good to see you too. You win another case?"

Jake's eyes softened, and his wide smile reached up to the corner of his eyes. "A couple, but we are just here for the sake of being here. What about you?"

"Greg wanted to grab a couple of drinks because it was Monday, and I couldn't pass up that opportunity."

"Great minds think alike. That is crazy. But, hey, you guys want to sit with us?" Jake offered while gesturing toward Dave and Samantha at a bigger table by the opposite wall.

"We wouldn't want to impose, would we, Stace?" Greg said.

Stacey noticed Greg was standing a little too close to her, but she focused on Jake's brown eyes when she said, "I would love to. Do you know what's good here? I'm starving."

Jake's smile grew twice its size, and he directed her toward their table, raving about the loaded Tater Tots.

Three hours later, everyone said their goodbyes, but Jake and Stacey stayed behind for a moment. Greg kept checking his watch every two seconds while Stacey and

Jake continued their seemingly never-ending conversation on how the beach is better than the woods.

"Don't you think you better be heading home soon, Stacey? We do have work in the morning," Greg said impatiently.

Out of the corner of her eye, Stacey saw Greg preparing to reach for her, so she stepped away just as his hand was about to make contact. "I'll be fine. See you at work tomorrow?" she said with the woman-to-woman "leave me alone" eye thing that Greg hated.

His nostrils flared, and with a simple "Yep, have a good night," he spun on his heels and walked out of the bar.

Stacey looked back up at Jake with a lighthearted chuckle, which he returned with a slight grin.

"You know, he is right; we should head home so we aren't too bad off for work tomorrow. But, hey, is there any chance…before you go…could I have your number? I would really like to see you again…on purpose next time," Jake asked falteringly and with a faint blush by the end.

It took everything in Stacey not to drop her jaw, so she used that energy to give him a small nod and a stuttered yes.

He passed his phone over to her, and she added in her number, but it took her a couple of tries; Jake hovered over her, and she shook in anticipation and nervous. They said their goodbyes and walked down the sidewalk in opposite directions, and as she was about to turn the corner toward the subway entrance, her body started to buzz. She didn't realize at first that it was the phone in her hand.

Hey, it's Jake. It was nice seeing you tonight. Hope you make it home all right

She froze on the first landing down the subway station's stairs and reread the message three times. A shiver ran up her spine, and her cheeks warmed. She started to type out a reply, but a small group of guys rushing down the steps almost pushed her down the next flight of stairs.

"Hey, watch it, assholes," she yelled down to them.

Two mocked her, and one raised his middle finger over his shoulder at her.

She let out an exasperated huff and tramped down the rest of the stairs.

The subway car was rather empty for that time of night, so she sat in the middle of a cluster of seats and pulled her phone back out as the doors closed, and the train started to roll forward.

It was nice seeing you tonight too, she typed. Her thumb hovered over the simple smiling emoji and the blissful, eyes-closed emoji, unsure if it would be too forward to go with the latter. *Fuck it,* she thought and pressed the cuter of the two.

In a matter of seconds, his read receipts popped up, and the typing bubble hovered for a moment.

It's so refreshing talking to someone who's funny and genuinely cheerful. I really didn't want to say goodbye if I'm being honest

Her heart flipped, and she smiled sheepishly to herself.

"Hey, you trippin'? Don't want no tweaker on this train; got my kid and too many groceries on me to fight a bitch off me if they havin' a bad trip," a woman a few years older than Stacey yelled at her from a cluster of seats across and over from her.

"I'm not tweaking, but thank you for minding your own business," Stacey replied.

The woman's mouth fluttered open and closed a couple of times as her eyebrows stitched together in confusion and indignation. "Watch yourself," the woman finally said in a soft but firm tone as she leaned back into her seat.

Stacey bristled for a moment as her nerves settled from the sudden burst of courage and audacity that came out of nowhere. She took a couple more breaths and looked back down at her phone.

It's because I was finally able to have a decent conversation with someone who's smart and, if I might add, a little dorky, she replied, ending it with an old fashioned :P, not an actual emoji.

The train slowed, and once she realized it was her stop, she grabbed her purse and took two strides to get to the doors. The doors opened, and she was immediately reminded of why she hated taking the subway during the summer. She rushed up the stairs, trying her hardest not to breathe through her nose, and panted semi-fresh air in and out once she made it to the street. It was still bustling in the usual Manhattan style.

Three blocks and two turns later, it was blissfully quiet in front of Mary's apartment building. Stacey walked into the apartment and found Mary sprawled out on the couch, watching the newest medieval magic show everyone was talking about, not because it was based on a popular video game, but because the main character was so inhumanly attractive. She had the TV at full volume, and it just so happened to be right at the point in which the hot lead reunites with the equally attractive love interest in a not-so-PG manner.

"I feel like a kid sitting next to my parents when a sex scene pops up on the screen," Stacey said as she closed the door.

Popcorn sprayed over the back of the couch, and Mary let out a small shriek. "Jesus, woman. You need a bell around your neck or something."

"You'd like it too much," Stacey retorted.

Mary shrugged her shoulders in acceptance and began cleaning up the popcorn minefield on the floor around the couch. "And what brings you home so late this fine eve, sloot?"

"It's nice that they fixed the AC. I don't know if I would have made it another night of sleeping in a sauna."

Mary snapped her fingers in front of Stacey's face as she sat on the arm of the couch.

"Hey, hey, hey! Don't go changing the subject at hand. Who was it this time?"

"Jake."

"J, that's a new letter. I don't think you've told me about a Jake. Did you meet up with him on your way home from work or something?"

"You could say that," Stacey said, playfully dangling the details in front of Mary, enjoying watching her squirm in anticipation and impatience.

"You are a G, you know that? What are you waiting for? Add it to your list!" Mary said as she almost fell off the couch while reaching for the piece of paper on the coffee table.

"Not yet, I wanna see how things go with him. Did I not tell you about him the first time I met him?" Stacey said as she genuinely thought about it.

Mary gaped at her and splayed her fingertips across her bosom.

"The woman was too stunned to speak," Stacey said.

"Well, I never!" Mary drawled in full old-school Southern-belle style.

"I'll take that as a no. So," Stacey started with a clap of her hands, "he is actually a friend of Greg's, and we met at this dive bar that Greg goes to all the time. It was actually that night I strolled in at, like, two in the morning, but that's a completely different story," Stacey rushed to get out as Mary's eyes bugged out of her head in surprised confusion.

"Oh, we are *definitely* backtracking to that story right here and now. Let me get the wine."

CHAPTER
16

This sunset was insane. Granted, I had a joint before chilling to watch it, but still

Stacey internally and externally groaned as she read the message from Travis.

"That's what your mom said last night," Mary said from her bedroom. She walked out and paraded her college sweat shorts and matching holey T-shirt after changing into them from her pencil skirt, button-down, and three-tiered gold statement necklace that matched her slim belt, which was threaded through the two decorative belt loops of the skirt.

"She's out of your league," Stacey said.

Mary mimed getting shot in the chest twice in response.

"Also, quite the wardrobe change." Stacey had opted for the Walmart jersey-knit skater dress that had yet to fail her.

"I know I'm femme, but, fuck, that shit is tiring."

"That's just being a woman in general. I'm surprised you haven't gotten used to it by now."

"My period reminds me of that enough, fuck you very much."

"No, but seriously, isn't Friday usually date night with you and Krista?"

"She's actually out of town for work for the weekend, so that means I get to binge-watch more magic Netflix shows without someone asking me what's going on every two seconds," Mary said passive-aggressively.

Stacey returned it with an open pursed lip. "That's such a masc thing to say though. Are you sure you aren't secretly masc?" Stacey asked.

"I enjoy my skirts too much. But let's reroute this convo to go over what you are currently wearing. That's your 'easy to turn on and take off' sundress. Who is it tonight?"

"Beach Travis."

"See, I told you he was still interested! It's been like a week, and he's still messaging you."

"They are still few and far between, and some of the messages don't really have much to go off of to continue the conversation."

"You aren't giving him the chance. What if he's better at talking in person, not over text message? You guys have a date tonight then?"

"Yeah, it's going to be pretty low-key. I guess he knows of a good fish-fry spot near him, and we are gonna do, like, a picnic at a local park too."

"That sounds like it'll be cute. You better give him hell and something that'll make him remember you. And hopefully something memorable enough that you always think about it when you look at the list."

* * *

Stacey trotted next to Travis as they walked back from the park, to his place, as the sun started to set. "That's a nice little spot. I'll have to keep that in mind if ever I'm in the area again."

"It really is. I grew up in the area, so I went there all the time when I was younger. The number of kickball games I won there... I should have gone pro," Travis said.

Stacey chuckled with him.

They turned a corner and walked toward a cluster of condos with little gardens in the small patch of "yard" in front of each unit. Some of them had their garage doors open to showcase a second living room with beat-up couches, bookshelves, and entertainment systems.

"People have some nice den garages around here. The fact that there is space for garages to be made into dens or second living rooms kinda makes me miss upstate."

"What part of upstate are you from?" Travis asked. They slowed, and he directed them toward one of the middle units that had a tasteful garden banner post that said "Welcome" and had sunflowers painted on it.

"Just west of Albany," Stacey said. She looked around the small porch to see a folded lawn chair in the corner.

"Oh, I'm horrible with decorating, so I grabbed the cheapest chair I could, and my mom got that for me," Travis said while he gestured over his shoulder at the flag as they walked into the apartment.

Stacey blushed in embarrassment as she realized her face must have made it a little obvious that she was silently judging. "It was the sunflowers that threw me off. You're not a fan of any sports teams or anything?" she said to backtrack in her defense.

"I watch, but I don't really follow any of them. If I'm not playing a pickup game of something at the park, I'm usually playing it on my Xbox."

As if on cue, Stacey looked into the living room and saw a meticulously set up entertainment center that had the DVDs, Xbox games, and Blu-ray disks perfectly categorized. "Shit," Stacey muttered under her breath. Her eyes floated from the living room to the little kitchen and saw that it was just as clean and meticulous, save for the mail he must have thrown on the table after grabbing it earlier in the day. There weren't too many other things in terms of decorations.

Travis sheepishly scratched the back of his neck as he watched her looking at everything. "Like I said, I'm not the best at decorating, but I like everything to be clean and in its place, so I like to say it's, like, minimalism to try to stay trendy."

"I could learn a thing or two from you, if I'm being honest," Stacey said jokingly, but with a hint of sincerity.

Travis raised an eyebrow so fast that Stacey wasn't even sure she had actually seen it, but he responded, "Hopefully you can teach me a few things in return."

A sudden fluttering of butterflies made a quick trip between Stacey's chest and her thighs, and she busied herself with taking her sandals off to try to fend it off.

Travis traveled over to the fridge and pulled something out. Before he closed the door, he looked over his shoulder at her. "Can I get you anything to drink? I have water, bottles of tea, and beer."

"Beer sounds good, as long as it's cold."

"Of course, that's the only way I'll have it." He passed her a bottle as he walked into the living room. "Do you play any video games?" he asked.

"Not really. But I'm interested to see what kind of a movie collection you have," Stacey said. She walked over and started to look through the DVDs and then the Blu-rays, and made a couple of remarks regarding his complete collection of the Marvel Universe films, but also all the *Paranormal Activity* series.

"What can I say? I've got taste."

Stacey settled on the first *Avengers* movie and handed it over for him to set up. His finger brushed hers for a moment when she passed it off to him, and their eyes locked for a tense yet short second.

They settled on the couch a few minutes later, sitting in the center of their respective couch cushions next to one another, not to seem too forward.

Loki had just teleported through the portal generated by the Tesseract, and was glaring at everyone, sweat dripping down his face. To lighten the mood and to ease her anxiety due to the silence, she asked, "Have you seen that show on Disney Plus yet, the one where they have the different variants of Loki?"

"I have. It wasn't too bad. A little trippy at times, but good."

"I heard there's a crocodile variant of Loki, and they even kept his antler helmet thing on it."

"Yeah, it was one of a few of them. There was a female Loki too, which was weird."

She was momentarily taken aback that he seemed more accepting of an animal version of a fictional character than of a female version, so she said, "I guess if there can be a crocodile Loki, it's possible there is a female Loki."

"You're not wrong," he said with a small chuckle. He shifted a little in his spot and looked over at her. "You comfortable sitting like that? You know you can sit closer to me if you want," he said with an inviting arm over the back of the couch, opening up his side for her.

She paused for a moment, but ultimately decided to snuggle in with him. They adjusted a little bit more before finally settling in. She started to match his breathing and become wrapped in his fresh, masculine scent, which only had a hint of whatever his deodorant was; the rest was just him.

Her heart beat faster, making other areas of her body pulse when he started to slowly rub his hand up and down her arm, and finally to trail up to her hair and to the back of her neck. He started to play with her hairline and tickle the back of her neck, which made her suddenly realize the back of a knee didn't seem so weird for an erogenous spot, after all. She wasn't about to burst into a thousand gold coins, but she was pretty damn close to it.

"My apologies to Scott Pilgrim," she muttered softly underneath her breath.

"What?"

"That feels good. I don't think I've ever had anyone play with my hair before." She closed her eyes so all her focus was on every movement his fingers made at her hairline.

He started to sense her breathing change and slowly trailed his fingers up the back of her scalp and gripped her hair. When she released an aroused and startled gasp, he turned her head to face him, and his eyes flickered from her eyes to her lips. She sighed softly, and that was all the invitation he needed to crush his lips to hers. He leaned into her, and she realized when he came up for air that she was lying on her back. He gave her a sly, lopsided grin and, without another word, stood up, grabbing her hand on the way, and pulled her toward the bedroom.

CHAPTER 17

They caught their breath for a moment, looked at each other, and shared an approving, satisfied laugh. As soon as that subsided, Travis got out of the bed and started to get dressed.

In her post-sex glow, Stacey felt giddy; she crawled to the end of the bed, got in front of him, and hugged him around the waist. When she felt him stiffen and not return the hug, all of the happy vibes deflated instantly. She looked up and saw him give her a shrug before putting his shirt back on. Completely taken aback, she asked playfully, "I guess you're not much of a cuddler, huh?"

"Yeah, no. Not really. I've never really been a cuddler. Hell, I'm not even a fan of sharing the bed with anything other than a dog. I get too warm, and it makes it hard to sleep," he said matter-of-factly.

Her mood dampened more, but she shrugged it off with a humorless chuckle. "I can get that, especially in these summer months. You know what? It was fun, but I have work in the morning, so I better get going."

"But it's a Friday. I thought you said you work Monday through Friday."

"I have a weekend job at my friend's diner; I work the breakfast rush for her."

She rushed out while she scrambled to put her clothes on. She could feel his eyes on her with every move she made, and a web of embarrassed heat spread down her neck to her back and then to her fingertips. She walked out of the bedroom and fumbled to grab her phone and purse with hands that felt three sizes too big. With a less-than-enthusiastic goodbye, she rushed out of the house and down the street as fast as she could.

When she got to the corner, a wave of numbness washed over her, and as if on autopilot, she headed in the direction of the closest subway station, marched down the stairs, swiped her MetroCard, waited for the next train, and sat down, all without blinking once. She focused on one spot of ripped vein in the vinyl on the seat across from her and rag-dolled with each bump of the train, barely noticing how much the wheels squealed every time it stopped. When she finally looked out at one of the stops, she realized she had missed the correct terminal, so she ran out of the door right as it started to close, hiked up the stairs to the cooling summer-night's air, and walked a block to the blue train in order to backtrack to her stop on the green train's route.

* * *

The walk up to Mary's apartment seemed like a chore even though it was only a total of eight steps from the sidewalk to her front door. Stacey dropped her keys to the door, once it closed, and let them clatter onto the kitchen table. Mary paused the TV and watched every step Stacey took to an accent chair, and continued to observe Stacey as she sat and looked at the canvas wall art of the New York City skyline at night, hyperfocused on the tip of the Empire State Building.

"Hey, kiddo. Rough night? You're home a lot earlier than I thought you would be. I'm guessing it didn't work out too well?"

Stacey turned her head horror-movie slow toward Mary before she said, "I give up."

Thinking she was just being overdramatic, Mary waved a hand in dismissal and tsked. "That was a bit much. On the bright side, you've made it through over a third of the list so far! You can't quit now. Sure, it's going to have its rough patches because we both know men ain't shit—you more than me—but not all of them are going to be Mr. Darcys."

"Wasn't he a complete ass to her though?" Stacey said before rubbing her face with her hands. She felt the start of her makeup smearing, but she didn't care.

Mary leaned back on the couch while she thought about it for a second. "Huh, I think you're right. I never actually watched the movie, only all of the memes." She gave the back of her neck a sheepish scratch as she stood up.

"Why does it have to be so hard?" Stacey asked the ceiling.

Mary stopped midstride and strained to hear her. "What part?"

"The searching and the meeting and the finding out the hard way and the realization that maybe it's something that isn't meant for you?"

A sudden tremor bubbled up inside Stacey; it left her both shivering and frozen in place, all at once. It ran down her back and caught in her lungs, forcing her to draw shallow breaths. Her hands curled into fists, but not a drop of strength was cupped within them as Stacey tried to grapple with the word she was looking for to simplify everything she was thinking and feeling at that moment. She pushed through the humming growing in her ears and tried to focus on the whisper of the fridge opening and the clinking of glass bottle hitting glass bottle. She tried to push the word back down as it drew to the surface. But, like a freight train, it hit her square in the chest and squeezed her throat just as an allergic reaction makes you feel weak, helpless.

Unwanted. The voice that said it was hushed, like a summer breeze, but the word burned as bright as the largest star in the universe.

Stacey's chin dropped to her chest; the blood drained from her ears. But it wasn't enough to drown out the word that repeated as if a toddler were echoing a word they shouldn't have heard in the first place. *Unwanted, unwanted, unwanted,* the toddler droned on and on, and eventually the words melted, gradually morphing into different words: *Unwanted. You. Unwanted. Don't. Unwanted. Deserve. Unwanted. Love.*

Stacey blinked and realized a pool had formed on the collar of her dress, below a waterfall that hugged to the contours of her cheeks and neck. She drew in a ragged breath and released the sob she'd held.

"Stacey?" Mary asked. She quickly dropped the bottles on the coffee table and knelt on the floor in front of Stacey, to find tears falling down her pale face and a distant, glassy look staring back at her, as if Stacey were not even on this planet any longer. "Oh God, Stacey. Fuck. You okay? Talk to me." Mary placed her hands on Stacey's knees and squeezed in reassurance, letting Stacey know she was there.

Stacey responded with a hiccup.

Mary reached up to wipe away a fresh tear. "Oh, honey." She knee-walked to the side table on the other side of the chair to grab a box of tissues and held them under Stacey's face.

A flicker of light gleamed in Stacey's eyes, and she finally focused on Mary. A fresh sob tore through her, and she grabbed a tissue.

Mary stood up and hugged Stacey's shoulders. "I think this calls for something a little stronger," Mary finally said after holding Stacey silently for a few minutes. She walked over to the table where she had placed the hard ciders and put them back in their place in the fridge. With a lift of her heel, she grabbed the bottle of vodka from the top of the fridge and pulled two glasses from the cupboard. After a clatter of ice and a fizz of soda, she walked back over and handed one glass to Stacey.

"Now…tell me what happened."

CHAPTER
18

Stacey looked at her phone the next morning through *The Mist*-level fog in her eyes to see that Greg had texted her...at two thirty-six in the morning. Without reading it, she dropped her phone back onto the table and stumbled toward the bathroom. She opened the door of her bedroom and worried that the trip to the bathroom was all for naught when she saw Mary silently waiting outside of it, rubbing the sand out of her eyes.

"Good grief, a little warning would have been nice. It's too early for this heart attack," Stacey said with her hand to her chest.

Mary brought her hands up in surrender as they danced to trade places in the doorway. "I gotta go too bad to make any sudden movements. I'm sorry!" Mary yelled from the other side of the closed bathroom door.

Stacey clomped to the kitchen and, on autopilot, began making coffee. By the time Mary was out of the bathroom, Mr. Coffee was halfway done with his thing.

"Bless you, child," Mary said as she sat in the chair across from Stacey at the kitchen table.

"As proprietor of this libation, I get the first cup," Stacey said.

"Rude, but I accept the defeat."

A minute later, Mr. Coffee hissed and wheezed his last drop, and Stacey stood up and pulled two mugs from the cupboard above it.

Mary started sipping on her cup as Stacey looked in the fridge for chocolate liqueur.

"If you're looking for the 'special creamer,' I used the last of it the other night."

"Rude," Stacey said playfully.

She sat back down at the kitchen table, and they drank their coffee while nibbling on granola bars.

A thunderous rap on the door made them both jump.

"The fuck! It is ten in the morning on a Saturday. Who the fuck…?" Mary muttered as she stood up to answer the door. She opened it to see her landlord's son in the middle of taping something to her door. Her stomach dropped for a second.

He jumped back in surprise. "Oh! Good morning, Mary," he stammered.

Mary looked from his sheepish face to the paper taped to her door. "Hey, Brian. Uhhh, what's going on?"

Brian wrung his fingers as he looked down at his feet. "Look, Mary, I really hate to do this, but per your lease, you can't have another person living in the apartment with you if they aren't on the lease, and they can't be added after it's been signed," he stated.

Stacey stood up and, on trembling legs, walked closer to the door, even though she could hear every word that was being said.

"I remember that clause in the lease. Is that why you're here today?" Mary said.

"Unfortunately, yes," he said with a sigh of regret. "I know that you have had someone living here with you for the last month or so, and against my wishes, I gotta let you know that if they don't move out in a week, you will be evicted in a month." He winced in advance as he awaited her reaction.

"A week? That's it? In this city? That doesn't leave her with much time to find a place. Besides, it's not like she has been staying here for like five months; it's only been a month."

Brian brought his hands up in surrender and pulsed them as if he were trying to calm a horse. "I know. I know it's not fair, and you know how my dad is—always wants to give out any kind of punishment without doing the dirty work himself," he said as he gestured to himself.

"But I've lived here for years! I've always been on time with my rent, and I've never been loud. I can't say the same for the cliff-jumping kid that lives above me, but this just seems a bit unfair."

A pulse of anxiety burned through Stacey, and she held on to the counter as her mind Rolodexed through twenty different thoughts: how she felt terrible for putting her best friend through this, where in the hell she would be able to find a place at such short notice, if there was anyone else she could live with if she couldn't find a place in time, how much it would be for just a bloody deposit, and how the money she was spending on a storage unit could go toward an apartment. Her breathing quickened, and she almost didn't hear him continue as her ears rang louder and louder by the second.

"Trust me, I'm not enjoying this conversation right now. But it's a good thing I came because my dad never would have told you that if she signed a lease with us for another place within that time span, it counts," Brian said.

Mary held in whatever she was about to say next and made a couple of unintelligible sounds as she processed what he was saying. "Wait. So you're saying that if she was to go to the main office down on East Sixty-Third right now and signed a lease with you, she could stay here until that place was available, no consequences for anyone?" Mary asked.

"That's exactly what I'm saying. But you'll have to be there with her, so we have it on record that she was the one here, and we don't accidentally take further action with evicting you."

"How do I know you aren't just saying this as a ploy to get another paying tenant in one of your buildings?" Mary asked defensively.

Brian scratched the back of his neck for a moment while he thought about it. "I guess I can see your hesitation. But I swear this is legitimate. I do have it on good authority that one in this building will be open at the start of August."

"But isn't that—" Mary started, but Brian held up his hands to pause her.

Stacey's ears stopped ringing, but her pulse quickened as she saw Mary lean back a little as her eyebrow lifted in response to his indignation.

"I know it doesn't sound real, but trust me that if you just go to the office, you'll be fine. But you didn't hear any of this from me," Brian said in a rush. He sighed when Mary didn't say anything in response, so he gave a weak wave goodbye and walked out of the building.

Mary closed the door with a stiff arm and crossed her arms. "Well shit. There goes my plan to do nothing today," she said.

* * *

They took the elevator up to the tenth floor and lightly rapped on the glass-windowed door as they walked in. A woman was sitting at the front desk on her cell phone; she slowly looked up as they came closer.

"Hey, how can I help ya?" she asked in a heavy Bronx accent.

"We were wondering if there were any openings for an apartment coming up in the building I'm currently living in. My friend has been living with me for a month, and she needs to find an apartment," Mary said.

Stacey gave a little wave as the woman looked over at her. Her eyebrows knit together in confusion and then finally annoyance.

"Damn that boy. I know exactly who you are. Donnie will be available in a minute, and he can get you set up and settled then."

CHAPTER
19

"You still haven't texted me back," Greg whispered to Stacey when he passed behind her desk Monday morning.

Stacey did a panicked double take toward Lisa's desk and silently sent a grateful prayer, to whatever was listening, that Lisa was probably in the kitchen getting coffee. Her anxiety was tamped a second later when she looked around at the other neighboring coworkers who looked as if they hadn't even realized Greg had walked by them.

She glared at Greg as he sat at his desk and gave her hurt puppy-dog eyes. She pulled out her phone and sent him, *First off, you're lucky Lisa wasn't here to hear that. Secondly, it's hard to reply to a* hey how are ya *at 2:30 in the morning. Doesn't look so hot*, and to see how he would take her response, she watched his face as he looked at his phone.

His jaw tightened, and he put his phone on his desk and logged into his computer without looking back at her.

Affronted by his reaction, her jaw dropped, and her lips twitched ever so slightly.

"Trying to catch breakfast? Try using some venom if they are too fast," Lisa said as she sat at her desk with a fresh mug of coffee.

Stacey processed that for a second and gave Lisa a scrunched face of "what the fuck" proportions. "Did you... just say I was a snake?" Stacey asked while she replayed it in her head to make sure she'd heard it correctly.

"Uh, yeah?" Lisa said in disbelief that it had taken Stacey that long to understand her comment.

"It's kind of poetic having someone like you call me the snake, but go off," Stacey said as she turned to her computer and started going through her email.

"Well, I guess the saying 'it takes one to know one' is pretty true then."

It took everything in her to keep from jumping up and slapping Lisa in the face.

* * *

How was your day today? Jake texted her right at 5:00 p.m.

Stacey gave her phone a doofy grin before she responded, *Can I sue a coworker for slander?*

She walked to the elevators as she waited for the typing ellipses to change to an actual text bubble. The elevator doors started to close behind her, but a hand reached in at the last minute, and they creaked back open. After having almost been slapped because of where she was standing in the elevator, she was ready to give the owner of the offending hand a look that could kill their future grandchildren. Little did she expect that the look was already being mirrored on Greg's face as he stepped onto the elevator.

"Jesus, Greg, you almost smacked me!"

"Well, if you'd heard me calling out for you to hold the elevator, it wouldn't have been an issue."

"I didn't hear anyone say shit."

"Yeah, because you were too busy texting on your phone."

"Who are you, my boomer parent? Yes, I was texting."

"Who were you texting? Seemed pretty important if you responded back immediately," Greg said defensively and rather more aggressively than Stacey had ever seen or heard him be.

She shook her head to clear out her confusion and gave him an exasperated sigh. "Is this about me not texting you back over the weekend?"

"Seems like you already know."

"You texted me at a prime booty-call hour, and it didn't sound like it was an emergency. Excuse me for not wanting to take part in that when I wasn't in the mood," she shot at him.

It was his turn to be taken aback by her animosity, and a sheepish glaze fell over his eyes before he looked down at his feet.

"It wasn't an emergency, was it? It was exactly what I said it was, right?" Stacey asked, guessing what his reaction meant.

The elevator *ding*ed to alert all riders that they had reached the bottom floor, and the doors opened to two men waiting to get on. Without hesitation, Stacey walked out without looking back to see if Greg followed closely behind her or to wait for his answer.

When Stacey cooled down enough to realize she had passed the entrance to her subway, she mentally kicked herself for being so melodramatic and mean. Guilt washed over her as she replayed their altercation in her mind and realized how sad and ashamed Greg looked when she stepped off the elevator. *He didn't deserve that*, she thought.

She stewed over it for another block, and when she looked up to try to figure out where she was, she realized she was standing right outside a patio bar, complete with lo-fi hip-hop renditions of anything by Jimmy Buffett. She walked through the doors and into the modern interior that had Latin influences in the artwork and booth lamps against all the black-painted brick. She meandered to the most open spot in the bar, slammed her purse down, and hopped onto a stool.

A bartender came over and greeted her, "How are you this evening?"

"I've been better. Also, men suck," she said in a moment of brutal honesty.

The bartender chuckled and nodded her head in agreement. "Take it from me, I know," she said as she gestured toward the bar and its patrons.

Stacey gave her a grateful grin before she ordered a house margarita. Realizing she wasn't seeing red anymore and now had the chance, she pulled her phone out and read the message Jake had sent her.

As long as there is probable cause, sir

She silently chuckled to herself at his reference to one of her favorite shows.

I have cause. It is be-cause I hate her, she sent back, proud of herself.

Almost immediately, her phone buzzed with a response. *Phew, was worried you didn't know the reference and I sounded absolutely unhinged*

Unhinged would be the number of times I've seen that show

Depends, is it more than four times?

On second thought, I retract that, you do sound absolutely unhinged, she sent back with a crying-laughing face emoji. Then she sipped at her drink with a stupid grin on her face.

I should have kept that embarrassing fact in until the 3rd date

Withholding evidence is a criminal offense, she texted, momentarily hoping she had that right.

I object, your Honor, we are trying to impress the girl, not run her off

If she were alone at home, she would have shamelessly squealed, put her face in her hands, and giggled like a little schoolgirl. Any grown woman on the face of this planet always reverts into a tittering teenage girl when she has a crush, no matter how old she is. Instead, she set her phone on the bar softly and bit her lip as she reached for her drink. She tipped it back and realized that all that was left was ice and the slice of lime.

Before she had the chance to place the glass back down on the coaster, the bartender placed another margarita in its place. Dumbfounded and confused, she looked up at the bartender, who simply shrugged and said, "The gentleman at the end of the bar bought your next drink for you."

A flush of excitement washed through Stacey as a new first was checked off her list of life events: a mysterious stranger from across the bar bought her a drink. The tone of warning in the bartender's voice, however, tamped

Stacey's delight down as woman-to-woman survival instincts kicked in.

Stacey looked around the bar and caught the eye of a man looking at her expectantly. He raised his beer up in a distant "cheers." She picked up her glass and returned the gesture. In response, he gathered his beer and stood up.

Stacey started to panic and looked over at the bartender, hoping she could keep it from happening, but all she got was an apologetic head bow before the bartender walked away.

Stacey looked back over at the man and gave him a quick once-over to gauge how this interaction would go. He was a shorter but muscular man, and her eyes focused on the two gold chains around his neck and the golden chili pepper winking at her as it reflected the lights from the bar. She did have to commend him for how sharp he was dressed, complete with charcoal-gray dress pants, lilac-colored button-down, and clean black dress loafers.

He finally made it over, sat down next to her, and without preamble said, "Hope you don't mind me coming to say hello."

I do but go off, she thought. "Hey, no, not at all. How are you tonight?" she asked instead.

"A lot better now. The name's Nicky. What's your name?" he asked.

"Stacey. What brings you here?"

"I live in one of the apartments upstairs, so I come here every so often when I come home from work. It's nice being so close to home, ya know?"

"Helps save on a taxi or the train, I guess. Hopefully, work isn't too far away either."

"A few blocks over. Nothin' too bad."

"Same for me. I was actually on my way to catch a train when I ended up here."

"You gotta take a train to and from work? I bet that can get interesting."

"Sometimes. Just the other day I almost had a woman fight me because I was texting."

"Yikes." He chuckled. "So have you been here before?"

"No, actually. But it's a nice little spot. Which came first for you, the apartment or the bar?"

"The apartment. The bar was just a perk," he said. He finished his beer and caught the eye of the bartender. Without exchanging a word, she grabbed one from the cooler, flicked off the cap, and placed it in front of him.

"You weren't kidding about coming here regularly," Stacey said. She took another sip of her drink and started to question what the look the bartender gave her meant. "How long have you lived here?"

"Only a year. I wanted to get away from home and to be closer to work. Call me crazy, but I can't stand the subway."

"Oh? Where's home?"

"Staten Island, baby!" he said eagerly.

She was a little taken aback at the sudden rise in volume, but she managed to hide it with a long gulp of her drink. "Yeah, that would definitely make for one hell of a commute. Wouldn't it be the ferry at that point?"

"Yeah, and that's just as bad. Although, if there was a dock close to here, I would have driven myself," he said.

She had to do a mental double take to pick up on what he was saying. "You have your own boat?"

"I do. I figured with how close I lived to the water, there was no way I wasn't going to have a boat," he said.

She immediately realized the meaning of the look the bartender gave her. "That's pretty cool. Do you keep it at your parents' place then?"

"Yeah. I go home on the weekends and take it out for some fun; the weather has been perfect for it."

"Definitely. I had to go up to the Riviera the other weekend because it got too hot for me."

"You'll never get hot on my boat; the breeze is too nice and perfect."

"That does sound really nice." She glanced down at her phone and realized that there were three messages waiting for her, one from Mary and two from Jake. She didn't have the chance to see a preview of any of them, but she made it look as though the messages were delivering horrible news.

"I am so sorry; my sister is about to go into labor, and I need to be there for her. Her husband is deployed, and I can't let her have the baby alone. I am so sorry I have to go already. It was nice meeting you, but I need to go." Stacey gathered her purse, dropped a twenty-dollar bill on the counter, and waved a final goodbye as she came just short of actually running out of there.

She didn't attempt to look back at all until she had made it to the subway stairwell and was actually on the train itself. After taking a moment to mentally shake off the excess douchiness that had followed her from the bar, she finally looked down at her phone and read her messages.

What do you want for dinner? I'm craving pizza from Big Tony's, Mary had sent.

Stacey simply replied back with the pizza-slice and drooling-face emojis.

So what character would you say you are? Stacey sent to Jake.

I feel like I would be more like a Jim with a hint of Dwight. Jim may have the looks but Dwight is the one that actually has the jokes, Jake sent back.

She responded with the clapping emoji and *That's a tough act to follow. Maybe a Phyllis with a hint of Kelly?*

His texting bubble popped up, and a moment later his reply came through. *Phyllis truly was an underrated character and I sincerely appreciate that you choose such a great one. I will admit, I hoped you weren't going to say Pam*

Why, what's so wrong about Pam?

Too 2 dimensional. Besides, Phyllis is kind of a freak, he sent with a smiling sweat-drop emoji.

Her jaw relaxed, and she stared at her phone for a moment, stunned and caught off guard. She looked up and saw that the train was about to reach her stop, so she got up and stood right at the doors in order to get off before someone tried to rudely get on.

Two blocks later, she was at Mary's doorstep, and before she could get her key out to unlock the outer door, the phone in her hand buzzed.

I'm sorry if that was inappropriate, the message from Jake read.

"What's that look for? You look like someone just passed you a secret note in middle school," Mary said as a way of greeting when Stacey opened the door to the apartment.

Stacey's eyes focused and saw Mary and Krista sitting at the kitchen table with the top of the pizza box hanging over the side, not a plate in sight. She kicked off her flats, walked over to the couch to deposit her purse on one of the cushions, and circled back to the fridge to grab a spiked iced tea.

"Hellooo? Is there something you would like to share with the class?" Mary said through a mouthful of food.

Stacey finished making her spiked peach tea and sat in one of the chairs before she looked at Mary. "It's Jake."

"She sounds hideous," Krista said without missing a beat.

"Well, she's a guy, so…" Mary said.

"What is he wearing?" Krista asked Stacey, her eyes full of hope that she would finish strong.

"Uhh, khakis?" Stacey said, barely getting out the s before laughing.

"No, but seriously," Krista said as soberly as she could a minute later as she wiped a tear from her cheek.

"He is actually delicious."

"You have a picture?" Krista asked. She used the pizza crust to point at Stacey's phone, and some crumbs rained down on the table.

Stacey froze for a second when she realized that not only did she not have his picture, but she didn't know his last name, what football team was his favorite, or whether or not he was competitive about everything. She wanted to relish in how great that felt, but the weight of Krista's and Mary's expectant glares kept her talking.

"I don't, but I've already met him, if that counts for anything."

Krista made a show of thinking on it before shaking her head. "For you, maybe, but not for us. How do we know that it wasn't a beer-goggles situation? I'm just looking out for my boo."

"Hey!" Mary said.

"You know what I mean," Krista said. They gave each other air-kisses before turning their attention back to Stacey.

She purposely took a huge bite, dramatically chewed, and swallowed. "He is very real. I met him through Greg."

"Coworker Greg? The one you've been getting to know biblically?" Krista asked, not overly intrigued by the answer.

"Yes, that Greg. He's been acting weird lately, so I've kind of decided to nip that in the bud." She aimlessly took another bite.

Meanwhile, Mary and Krista exchanged a look that said, *Is this girl dense or something?* before looking back at Stacey expectantly.

"What?"

"How long would you say he's been acting weird?" Krista asked.

"Yeah, you hadn't brought any of this up before, so spill, woman," Mary said in follow-up.

"We ran into Jake at the bar a second time with his coworkers, and Greg has been short with me ever since."

"Was there anything that happened between you and Jake while you were with Greg?"

"I mean, we talked and had some side conversations. And then Jake gave me his number at the end of the night," Stacey said.

Mary and Krista both threw their arms up in exasperation.

Stacey jumped a little and slowly pushed her chair away from the table.

"As a woman, I am disappointed in you for not seeing the signs sooner. As a homosexual, I am distraught that I am picking up on moods from a guy better than you," Krista said.

"Hey now," Stacey said defensively. "No need to be nasty here. I obviously noticed something, but I didn't think it was about Jake. I thought it was about the fact that I hadn't really hooked up with him in a while without explanation."

"Yeah, no, that would do it too," Krista acquiesced.

"Now, I'm really curious to see what this man looks like. I wanna know just how 'straight' Greg is if he feels this threatened," Mary said.

"Aren't you the one that says that literally no one is one hundred percent straight, even the one's spouting all the Super Straight bullshit?" Stacey asked.

Mary just gave her a little wave as if brushing off what she just said and focused on the situation at hand. "I don't care how it needs to be done; we need to see a picture of this man."

"If I can find him on social media, will you get off my back?"

"We all have to make compromises at some point."

CHAPTER
20

Stacey swiped to the left on the third profile she stumbled across; it had the "best way to get to know me" prompt answered, "Just ask," punctuated with a winking-face emoji. It was only the tenth profile she had seen that day.

Annoyed at herself for even still entertaining the idea of finding a man in this dating climate, and after she had unofficially sworn off dating a lot sooner than she was willing to admit to herself, she closed the app. She placed her phone on the table with a dull *thunk* and looked down at her soup to take another bite.

The bell over the door to the café chimed, but she didn't give it a second thought as she dug into her Italian wedding soup.

"It is, like, ninety degrees outside. How are you eating soup right now?"

Her blood chilled, and her spoon froze in the air halfway between the cup and her mouth. She didn't need to look up to know exactly who had graced her with his appearance; her memory worked overtime as the scene from over a month before ran on a loop, complete with cigarette burn marks and record scratches, and started over again. She remembered all too well the way he looked down at her from the top of the staircase, pointing his finger at her, his self-preservation coming off as righteousness to justify what he had done.

The familiar burning sensation of tears thickened the back of her throat, but she pushed through it and attempted to come off as annoyed. She dropped the spoon into the cup and pushed it away as if she were done.

"Stacey," he said a little softer and sounding almost wounded.

Her heart skipped a beat, and she had to hold her breath for a second before she could look up into his brown eyes. She once saw them full of light and character, but now they were dull and thoughtless. *Fitting for them to be the same color as shit,* she thought to herself.

"What?" she spat as she glared up at Tyler and tried to portray as much venom as she could from her eyes, attempting to make him take the hint.

The first emotion she registered through the red haze that had filtered over her eyes was surprise, and immediately after she was able to see, to her satisfaction, pain.

"I just wanted to say that…"

"I thought we already went through everything that we could possibly have to say to one another. You know, back when you broke my heart and acted like it was all my fault," Stacey hissed. She could see a few heads from neighboring tables turn in her direction, but she had her tunnel vision set on his clenched jaw and wounded eyes.

"Jesus, Stacey, try not to make a scene." He shoved his hands into his pockets and rolled his eyes so far his head tipped back with the force of it.

"I thought we were just exchanging words. Those were the words I wanted to exchange with you," she said as she stood up. She left the rest of her lunch on the table and swung her purse over her shoulder with enough force to make sure it hit him as she passed.

The bell over the front door chimed once for her and then for him a second later.

"Stacey, wait!"

She kept her fast stride up as best she could to avoid all the people during the lunch-hour foot rush.

"Dammit, Stacey!" Tyler growled as he grabbed her left arm.

She whipped around to face him, tears streaming from her eyes, her blood boiling. Before she could think about what she was doing, her right hand flew out and landed flat on his cheek.

He stumbled away a few steps, and the other pedestrians suddenly stopped crowding her.

She shook her hand a couple of times to try to whip away the almost-numb stinging sensation that ebbed from her palm to her fingertips.

"Fuck. Ow!" Tyler grumbled as he tried to soothe the pain and bruise that was already forming right below his left eye. "I'm trying to have a civil and adult conversation, and you're throwing punches at me. What the fuck!"

She ripped her arm out of his hand and turned around to fully face him. "What a load of shit! Now you know how much it hurt, how bad it stung. I loved you! How dare you! How dare you act so selfish and then turn around to act like the mature one right now! Do you have any idea how selfish you are? Or how childish you were to not talk to me about anything before fucking around behind my back?" Stacey yelled. Tears openly streamed down from her eyes, and every breath she took made her waver from the effort.

Without missing a beat, he threw his hands up in defeat and rubbed the uninjured side of his face in exasperation. "And making a scene in the middle of the street is any better? Get your head out of your ass. I truly was hoping for a civil conversation," he shot back.

"No, all you were hoping for is the validation that all was fine between us. But all is not fine. I lost a home. I lost emotional security. I lost self-respect. I lost prime years of my life that I spent being with you that I can't get back. Do you know how much it hurts knowing how much of my life I have wasted trying to accommodate you, especially after realizing that it was all a fucking sham?" she cried out. Her tears had stopped flowing and had started to sizzle on her cheeks as his indignation made her hotter and hotter with anger.

"What about me, huh? I wasted the same amount of time as you did, you know. You don't think I wish to get those years back either?" he said, pointing at his chest over his heart, as if to emphasize he was hurting.

But she knew it was all an act; it was always an act. She squinted her eyes and stiffened her lips into thin lines. "I could give a shit about you. You know why? Because you already said it yourself; it was forced from the start, but you kept leading me on with your bullshit. I don't give a shit about the fake years you lost, because I lost real ones."

Tyler ran a hand through his hair in frustration, and it stuck up in odd angles as it fought against the way the gel had held it together up until that point. "What a fucking psycho! Are you kidding me?"

"No, I'm not, and I don't want to hear another word out of your mouth; I don't want to hear how much you're better off, or how it feels 'more genuine' with her, or whatever other sniveling you had rehearsed and up your sleeve. Go fuck yourself, your childish mentality that was holding me back, and your small dick. I faked it like eighty percent of the time, by the way," she said with a glance down toward his pants. She heard a scattering of gasps around her and a snicker as she turned and walked toward her office building, pushing through the mosh pit of rubberneckers and weaving in and out of the dispersing crowd.

As soon as the doors to the conveniently empty elevator closed, she released a wailing scream that lasted the length of three floors. As the doors to her floor opened, a few people were staring in her direction as if they had clustered near it to see who got off.

Lisa looked up as Stacey dropped her purse on her own desk and plopped down into her seat, followed by a *thunk* of her head on the desk, which was heard around the office.

"You're more melodramatic than normal today," Lisa said matter-of-factly.

"Shut up, Lisa," Stacey said to her lap.

"I didn't quite hear that. Should I keep talking about how you need to keep your drama out of work and at home?"

Stacey slowly raised her head and with the deadliest stare replied, "Shut. Up. Lisa. Was that clear enough to be heard from your ass? It's a terrible hat on you, by the way."

Lisa's jaw unhinged and she gasped at the air as if she were a fish out of water. "This may have been the last time you say anything to me," Lisa finally said as she stood up.

"If you tell on her, I'm going to be on her side," Greg said from behind Lisa. She whipped around, and Greg tried hard not to flinch at the fire in her eyes.

Stacey looked around Lisa and gave him a soft smile full of gratitude.

In return, he gave her a slight grin and the smallest of shrugs.

Someone from a row over stood up and after a pause said, "Me too."

The woman next to him stood up and said, "I'm on her side too."

A few more people piped up from behind those coworkers.

Lisa looked desperately from Stacey to everyone else who'd spoken up, and to the direction of Steve's office, and back again, before she sat back down in defeat.

Stacey looked back at her computer screen and had a hard time logging in due to the adrenaline-fueled shake in her hands.

* * *

"Best way to ask me out is to: Just ask me out"

Left Swipe.

"Best way to get to know me: Just ask. I'm an open book"

Left swipe.

Fish picture

Left swipe.

During a break from packing what she had at Mary's, Stacey had flopped onto the couch and aimlessly swiped through Tinder one last time to try. She wasn't sure if she wanted to seek validation, to humor herself, or to tamp out any underlying FOMO that might possibly be lingering in her system.

It wasn't until she stumbled across the most contradictory prompt that she wanted to throw everything out the window, She-Hulk smash-style.

"Worst Idea I've ever had: Signing up for online dating. Ha! Get it? It's ironic because I'm on a dating site"

"What's the fucking point then? Why go through the hassle? Why announce to every possible future partner that you have no interest in putting any effort into anything," she grumbled to the empty apartment.

Her head rolled to the side as she released a calming sigh, and the glint of the glitter on the list drew her eye in. She sat up, pulled it out from under a small pile of books, and smoothed it out in the center of the coffee table. The more she looked at it, the more she felt as if it were mocking her, judging her both for making it so far into the list and for how much she still had left to complete. Fifteen completed letters shone back at her like neon lights, and as she read each name, she was reminded of some emotion she couldn't quite pinpoint as her mind played out each interaction in agonizing detail. It wasn't until she got to letter *P* that she realized what that emotion was.

"Humiliation," she whispered out loud.

She pondered why she'd started the list in the first place and what she'd hoped would come of it. It all started and ended in humiliation.

And she hated it.

On her next breath, she reached for the list and just started ripping. There was no rhyme or reason in how it ripped; all she was focused on was the destruction.

As the red hue left her vision, she looked at the snow-fall of construction paper and glitter in front of her. Her breathing calmed, and she stood to start gathering the pieces that had landed on the floor. That's when she realized one letter was left untouched on the very top of the pile: *S*. She racked her brain, wondering how she could have missed such a common letter and why it felt as if she truly did forget to write a name down.

Tentatively, she grabbed the pen sitting on the table next to her and held it, thinking that would help spark whom exactly she was forgetting. One glance at the fidgeting hand, and she knew exactly what name she needed to put there.

She stood and, with a proud grin, admired the cursive and the boldness of the name written in front of her: "Stacey."

EPILOGUE

"I really wish more apartment buildings had elevators because having to lug up a mattress, the frame, and a bloody couch is just cruel, and may actually be an interrogation tactic the FBI uses. Prove me wrong," Mary groaned, and she flopped onto the mattress on the floor of Stacey's bedroom. Stacey hadn't put together the frame yet, so the mattress sat at a weird angle on the box frame on the floor.

"You and me both. I'm also glad your apartment is on the first floor because I honestly can't fathom having to do this again when you decide to move out of your place," Krista said from the couch on the far side of the living room.

Stacey made a mental note of just how much extra work she had ahead of her, putting the currently scattered pieces of furniture in the right places. With the bed and the couch occupied, Stacey opted for one of the dining table's chairs.

"I really do appreciate you two helping me out with this. Between the heat, the stairs, and the running back and forth from the storage unit, it's definitely going to be a bubble-bath-type night," Stacey said.

She heard a surround-sound "amen" before a fit of giggles, pinches, and pokes thrown back and forth between Mary and Krista.

* * *

Later that night, Stacey was working on the wall decorations before setting the furniture in order. She had made a statement wall above where she planned to put her shorter bookshelves and was starting on the small wall that would sit behind the couch. She had just hung the decorative mirror when her phone buzzed on the coffee table.

"Hello?" she answered.

"Hey, Stacey. I was, uh…just wondering if you, uh… if you had dinner yet?" Jake asked from the other end of the connection.

An enamored little grin lit up her face, and she had to hold back every urge to do a giddy little dance. "Hey, Jake. No, I haven't actually. Just been busy moving into my new place."

"Oh my goodness, that's right! If you aren't too tired, can I treat you to dinner, and then you can tell me all about it?"

At that, Stacey couldn't hold back that dance before she answered with a "That sounds really good."

"Great! How does Ryan's on 153rd at eight sound?"

"That sounds perfect to me. I'll see you then."

She hung up and clutched the phone to her chest for a moment before she set off on the fastest shower known to man, put her hair up in a cute but messy bun, and applied a little bit of makeup to cover the bags that had formed from all the moving that day.

After she was dressed and had grabbed her wallet from the coffee table, she caught her reflection in the decorative mirror and was excited to see the easy and natural happy glow reflected back at her, a glow she hadn't been sure she would ever see again.

She blew her reflection a kiss and floated out of her apartment.

BONUS CONTENT

We have all been there, glaring at that rom-com through teary eyes, eating a box of chocolates *Legally Blonde*-style. But instead of throwing away the box and wasting any raspberry-filled chocolates, check out this list of some dos and don'ts of postpartum from your ex-bae.

A. We are all adults here, and we all know that *A* is for **alcohol.** This isn't *Sesame Street*, but there are still some lessons we'll need to teach you.

Do: Have some girl-power happy hours because your posse is *the* best source of positive vibes now that you've lost all that dead weight.

Don't: Use alcohol to make everything seem a bit better. Once you start thinking, "I'll have more at home after I finish my second round of two-for-one, happy-hour drinks," you may need to have a talk with your girlfriends, or they will be having *the* talk with you.

B. Of course, this is for **beaches**, bitch. If anything, think that this breakup happened at the best time because you, for sure, deserve a hot-girl summer.

Do: Walks on the beach by yourself; they are peaceful as hell. Try it sometime. But having a day out with a snuck-in cooler of hard seltzers and getting a naughty little tan line is better and hotter than every bed romp you had with your ex, and you can even make it last longer than five minutes.

Don't: Go a bit ham on the freedom high, as tempting as it may be. Always make sure you pair up with your girlfriends if going to a midnight beach party to which some random guys on a docked boat invited you. Need I f*cking say more?

C. As simple as it is, there will always be a good and acceptable time for **cuddles**. Simple, we know, but remember that humans crave touch just as much as food, and some people can live on a vegan diet.

Do: Be open honest with hookups or prospective new partners that you just want to Netflix and Cuddle, not Hulu and Do You. The new normal—cuddling doesn't always have to turn into sex.

Don't: Cuddle with someone you don't know, but always make sure you're sober because men suck sometimes.

D. Besides sex, this is our favorite form of cardio: **dancing**.

Do: Go to your favorite club in an outfit that makes you feel like the bad bitch you are, or have a sleepover-style dance party, minus the brother and friends in dresses. Unless it's a drag bar, then rock the shit outta that. Also,

Just Dance is popping up on most gaming platforms in digital format, and it is compatible with smartphones, so rock to some classic mid-2000s' pop, or get down with some Just Dance classics.

Don't: Get sloppy in the club. I feel as if I don't have to say more. If your girlfriends don't stop you, that speaks even more volumes.

E. Like any quitter of an addiction, the best way to get over it is to get away from it. Kicking your ex out of your four-story walk-up is step one in **escaping** the mundane.

Do: Use up some of that PTO. You have the right to use time that you've earned; the job will be there when you get back. Find a spa a couple of towns over and stay for the weekend, or if your parents are snowbirds, you're never too old to crash on their couch and save on an Airbnb.

Don't: Drop everything on the spur of the moment and take a trip to a country where only like 35 percent of the population can help direct you around the city. As tempting as it would be to live up to the glorious and timeless Julia Roberts, your landlord won't be happy, and your apartment will *not* be the way you left it four missed rent checks ago.

F. No, these aren't the two words you will say to your ex any and every time you see them after the breakup. This is a lot more powerful: **Family**.

Do: Take the time to make up for any missed opportunities with your blood because you "had a thing with your ex" and couldn't make it. Besides, your mother will *always* know what comfort food you will need at any given time.

Don't: Revert back to the high school you and take out any frustrations you may have on your parents because "they just don't understand." Listen here: Grow up. They do understand.

G. Let's not beat around the bush about shared interests you had with your ex, especially the types of video **games** they played. No first-person shooters revolving around a world war or taking down a cult in the woods here, babe.

Do: Play any of the growing genre of games known as "cozy games." They range from the classic Stardew Valley and Minecraft, all the way up to Animal Crossing and that one in which you unpack boxes and organize a room.

Don't: Go on a Sims bender and have your friends find you in a blanket cloak with empty Doritos bags scattered on your bed, hunched over your laptop, leveling up your sixth adopted cat to be the head ghost hunter.

H. This may sound obvious, but in the end, you just need to **heal**. It'll seem hard and impossible at times, but we know how strong you are.

Do: Do some meditating and yoga; it'll help balance you spiritually, which will help you emotionally, which in turn will help you mentally.

Don't: Keep tabs on them, scrolling through their social media accounts to see what they have been up to. They aren't your responsibility anymore, and it will just make it harder to let them go.

I. With new friends, time, and change of scenery for your day-to-day, think back and see if there are any **interests** that you have been putting on the back burner because it wasn't something your partner was into, or there wasn't space for it in the apartment you shared.

Do: Pick up that crochet hook, that paintbrush, that puzzle, and get back into it. It might seem hard at first, but once you get that sweet hit of serotonin back, you'll never want to stop it again.

Don't: Equate the last part of this tip to drugs. Look how strong and successful you are now, after being sober for so long. Imagine how much stronger you will be when you can keep adding years to that accomplishment.

J. Sometimes the weirdest things have some sort of connection to your ex: that park where you had that picnic, a holiday drink that you shared, or even something deeper, like finances. If that's the case, get a fresh start with a new **job**, one that a bad bitch like you deserves. Making a better life for yourself might be just what the doctor ordered.

Do: Search for jobs that are closer to your interests, so it doesn't feel like a drag, and that have better benefits; there's always a better office out there for you.

Don't: Work yourself to the bone with overtime or with a second job. There are healthier avenues of escapism, and as they say, "I ain't never seen a hearse with a trailer hitch."

K. There are plenty of things that can come out of a relationship: heartbreak, a gnarly STD that your ex never told you they picked up from the other person, a new lease on life, and in some cases, **kids**.

Do : Establish a healthy visitation schedule or shared parenting, and make sure you continue to love your children unconditionally and to help them understand.

Don't: Ever trash talk the other parent—this goes for both sides. N take out your frustrations on your children or put them on the back burner while you make your way through your new Tinder profile. They are symbols of the love that you can give the world and the future; you don't need to be traumatizing them.

L. This article wouldn't have come full circle if this letter weren't **Lists**. It may sound stupid and elementary, but it may be the best thing for you to do to get your mind off things when things seem to get a little dark.

Do: Make a list. It could focus on a specific topic or just be random doodles, Robert California from *The Office*-style. Start off with something simple, like your favorite desserts or dream jobs or animals, that starts with the same letter as your name. Bonus round if it's a to-do list of sorts and you finish it because you're a bad bitch.

Don't: Make a hit list. It's not cute, and it's really creepy. Just don't do it.

M. This one is for **Me time**, because of course it is!

Do: Make sure you are getting back to your own roots and doing what you love to do. Remember that you love walking along the river, and your ex wanted to walk through their Xbox achievements? Do it! It'll give you some fresh air, rev up some endorphins, and allow you to see just how strong and independent you are.

Don't: Retreat into yourself. Stewing about "I could have done things differently" or "I should have seen the signs" scenarios isn't healthy, and you are at your best when you're healthy.

N. There are a couple of healthy ways to partake in escapism, and sometimes just picking up a **novel** and getting back into a genre you loved before or a romance a la characters of Lyssa Kay Adams can do you a world of good. Go for it.

Do : Read. That's pretty self-explanatory.

Don't: Make excuses to avoid reading.

O. For some of you, this one might be hard, especially depending on the reason for the breakup, but this will help in the long run: be **open-minded**.

Do : Be the bigger person. It's okay to have animosity toward your ex, but if they want to state their piece, let them. This lets you be the bigger person, and deep down it'll help both of you get some closure.

Don't: Fall for their words if they try to reconcile. Some things are best left in the past.

P. We understand that getting out of some relationships can be extremely hard because of extenuating circumstances, but we just want you to know that we are **proud** of you. You are so strong, and we are so happy to see you finally be able to hold your head up high, you bad a-f boss woman.

Q. This one isn't really a tip, but more of a reminder: You are a **queen**.

Do : Stay strong and slay each day.

Don't: Forget it.

R. Being single can be hard for some gals; we get that. But when it's time to get back out there, make sure you are **ready** and are on the lookout for the best of possible suitors.

Do: Wait. We get lonely and sometimes mistake a craving for a genuine connection. We don't want to see you get hurt again, Queen.

Don't: Log back into all your old profiles with all the same prompts and pictures; that's how you got the last one, more than likely. You are a new person with a new lease on life; you should look for a new partner who values that in you.

S. This is one of our personal favorites on this list. We all think we are the best at this, but there's no harm in getting in some more practice when it comes to **sex**.

Do : Have sex if you happen to hit it off with that one person at the bar and things lead to the bedroom; don't be afraid to try something you hadn't with your ex, be it a position or dirty talk or just straight communication. If it's because you have a hard time finding your sweet spot, we wholeheartedly believe in self-practice. We would be happy to provide a separate list of bed-side-table-drawer essentials.

Don't: Go at it blindly and unprotected. We are all about letting your freak flag fly, but STDs can put a real damper on things. Also, make sure you are safe with the partner you have selected that night. Girl code is letting your friends know where you are when you are with a new partner, even if it's just on a date at a local bar.

T. With the extra time on your hands, **try** some new things.

Do : Take a cycling class or do a Painting with a Twist. If you aren't much of a painter, then find a place that does trivia nights or axe throwing.

Don't: Use this as a chance to become a daredevil. Unless you have actually always wanted to go skydiving or something as daring, start small.

U. Tap into that empowered side of you and **undress** yourself. It will leave you bare in both the literal and meta-phorical sense for when you are ready to get back out there, thereby giving you the chance to open up to people more.

Do : Walk around your place naked whenever you are home or to take it a step further, go commando for a day and unshackle yourself from the confines of underwear.

Don't: Streak. It's not exactly legal, and we can't afford to pay your bail.

V. This one is a great one for everyone involved: **volunteer**. It's a great chance for you to get out, meet new people, and help the community you live in.

Do: Look up your local soup kitchens or animal shelters and help out in any way that you can.

Don't: Do it just because you know one of the organizers is hot, and you wanna hit that. Here's looking at you, Samantha!

W. This is one of those things that is uncomfortable to talk about, but it needs to be said nonetheless; please **wash** yourself. We know it can be hard at this point in time, but for the love of all that's good, please listen to us.

Do: Stock up on lavender bath bombs. Think of it as a symbolic way of "washing" them out of your life with every bath or shower you take.

Don't: Stock up on baby wipes and body spray. Everyone knows, even if you have your hair in a bun every day.

X. We've got nothing for this letter, and our editor won't allow us to include Xanax. *You* try to think of a cute way to include xylophone or X-ray in a self-empowerment article. Take your time; we'll wait.

Y. This is for our former long-term relationship babes, especially the high school sweethearts. If any of the musicians' albums with a reference to their age has taught us anything, sometimes we lose a bit too much of our **youth** when in serious relationships at a young age.

Do : Get that Loungefly purse of your favorite Disney princess, or play on that public playground, no pun intended, at two in the morning. Take the time to reclaim some of those little pieces of youth that you didn't have the chance to partake in when you needed to be a forty-year-old at the age of twenty.

Don't: Act like a toddler, and have tantrums in public. Leave that to the Karens.

Z. All in all, we just want you to get back your **zest** for everything: life, love, the world, yourself.

Do : Be unabashedly positive that if you follow this DO list, you will come out the other side as your favorite version of yourself.

Don't: Overthink it. Just breathe and live; that's all we ask.

LET'S CONNECT

Find out more about Alma Hulbert at the following links!

Email: almahulbert@gmail.com

TikTok: @alma.writes.stuff